D1503812

Books by Michael Mewshaw

MAN IN MOTION

WAKING SLOW

THE TOLL

EARTHLY BREAD

EARTHLY BREAD

EARTHLY BREAD

by

Michael Mewshaw

Random House · New York

Published in the United States by Random House, Inc., New York, and simultaneously in Canada by Random House of Canada Limited, Toronto.

Library of Congress Cataloging in Publication Data

Mewshaw, Michael, 1943–
Earthly bread.
I. Title.
PZ4.M597Ear [PS3563.E87] 813'.5'4 76–7991
ISBN 0–394–49925–5

Manufactured in the United States of America

24689753

First Edition

For

THOMAS, JR., EUNICE, THOMAS III

and

NANCY TROWBRIDGE

"Thou didst promise them the bread of Heaven, but I repeat again, can it compare with earthly bread in the eyes of the weak, ever sinful and ignoble race of man? And if for the sake of the bread of Heaven thousands and tens of thousands shall follow Thee, what is to become of the millions and tens of millions of creatures who will not have the strength to forego the earthly bread for the sake of the heavenly?"

—Fyodor Dostoevsky, *The Brothers Karamazov*

EARTHLY BREAD

Prologue

The subway car shuddered and swayed as it passed under the city, shooting sparks from its rusty tracks. The heat was infernal, the smell sulfuric, as if the floor were on fire. Spectacular graffiti covered the car—not just the predictable obscenities, but strange codes, symbols and mystical numbers, as though deep underground a tribe of artist-insurrectionists were plotting revolution. I had been holding the *Daily News* like a shield in front of my face, but then let it crumple to my lap, a swollen print of my sweaty fingers on the page.

CHURCH ADJUSTS TO CHANGING ROLE, read the headline under a hemorrhoid ad ("Do you suffer from painful elimination?"). "The hormones used in manufacturing fertility drugs are extracted from the urine of middle-aged and elderly women, and fortunately for the Catholic Church the most convenient source seems to be convents. As one enterprising bishop put it, 'Our aim has always been to please. I know the nuns, in a spirit of Ecumenicism, are delighted to learn they're doing their part. Of course, this also helps with our budget problems.' "

So it had come to that, I thought. Urine was all the Church had to offer. Suddenly, I experienced a sharp empathy with an old man across the aisle. His face frail and refined, he appeared to notice nothing of his surroundings, and yet every few minutes he shrugged and raised his hands as if to ask, "What's the use?"

Next to him, a young girl wore a loosely woven pullover that resembled a fishnet someone more modest had draped over her bare torso. Her boyfriend—I hoped that was who he was—had leaned close, and with no pretense of secrecy caressed her breasts. Two startled pink buds poked through the mesh, and as the car swerved around a corner they rocked back and forth, paralleling the sweep of her bored eyes.

Unaccountably, in that cauldron of a subway car, I shivered. Dressed in olive-drab pants and a mustard-colored shirt, I was anonymous, yet there was no need to speculate how the kids across the aisle, the old man or the other riders might react if I interrupted and introduced myself as Anthony Amico, a priest, a Paulist father. They'd only glance up in mild surprise, wondering whether I was dangerous and if it was possible that someone still believed.

I had seen such reactions even in Rome, where during my year of rest and recuperation I had said Mass in basilicas throughout the city. At the Consecration, as I elevated the Host and peered over the altar at the congregation, I always noticed several black-shawled shriveled old ladies praying in the hard wooden pews while all around us lurked Germans in lederhosen, Japanese carrying cameras, and Americans with ice-cream cones and copies of *Europe on $5 a Day.* They regarded us and what I was doing with wry curiosity, as one might stare at an Indian, some sad, shabby dipsomaniac lurching through a half-remembered rain dance, hoping the tourists will toss him quarters.

The train stopped, and I got off and hurried toward the stairs, past the riveted pillars and pipes dripping grimy perspiration. It was foolish to slow down, frightening to stand still.

When everybody moved at the same time in the same direction, there was at least the illusion of order. But whenever I hesitated and others stumbled by, thrown off balance and cursing, I was shaken by the lemming-like rush, and all my senses seemed abnormally responsive. I was vulnerable to the lightest touch, to the least change in temperature, sound or smell. Perhaps I was still suspended in jet lag, or suffering a kind of reverse culture shock after Rome.

But there were memories, too, to torment me, for I was well aware of what it meant to stop, to grind to a halt like Lot's wife. One morning more than a year ago, I had left the parish church and started across the recess yard toward the bus station, half-listening to the children inside the school chant their catechism in cadence to my footsteps. I had just finished Mass and was on my way to a department store to pick up the uniforms for our CYO basketball team when I stopped to ponder a problem I was having.

The problem was whether I was losing my mind or my faith. I had begun to suspect I was going crazy from trying so hard not to go crazy—and not to leave the priesthood. I kept telling myself the important point was to get to the store, to pick up those uniforms, and later I would work my way beyond this spiritual impasse. But I couldn't make myself move, not even when the children raced out after lunch and discovered me standing there stiff and straight as a tetherball pole. They were hollering "Be on my team, Father Tony" when Sister Brenda Marie saw something was wrong, shooed the kids back into the building and sent for the pastor, who, after failing to get me to speak, called the rescue squad.

The pastor—and several psychiatrists in New York City and Rome—later referred to this as a breakdown, but I took some pride in the fact that I never collapsed altogether. I remained upright, and for months afterward I lumbered along resolutely, going without complaint wherever I was ordered, answering without hesitation every question I was asked. Yet, although I had no reluctance to admit I was sick (years under the yoke of obedience had had their effect and confession had prepared me for the personal revelations of therapy), I found it difficult to explain why I felt like a spare part for a machine that had been declared obsolete or like one of those phantom limbs amputees complain about, an ache where an arm no longer existed.

When I reached street level, a tank truck was rumbling up the avenue, buffing the asphalt, and I caught a cool spray on my arms. Then the clammy evening closed around me, and I felt a different spray, the tepid drizzle from window air conditioners high overhead.

I stepped close to the curb, eying each passer-by. I had lived in the city almost all my life, yet after a year in Italy—where I could walk anyplace in safety—I feared everyone on the West Side meant to mug me. My brother Lenny, always better equipped to protect himself, had taken to carrying a pocket-size transistor radio, and at the first sign of trouble he whipped it out with a flourish, extended the antenna and shouted, "Four-oh-six, we've got a ten-thirteen in progress on West End Avenue! Send a squad car pronto!"

That cleared his path, he claimed, and was lighter, safer and less expensive than packing a .38. Plus you could listen to the ball games. But with my luck, I'd cross the one nut in New York who had sworn to kill the next person he spotted with a portable radio.

I did suck in my stomach, however, striving for a show of force, but it was a pathetic showing, since for each certainty I had lost, I seemed to have gained a pound of fat. In the morning, when I scraped off the shaving cream, I scarcely recognized my own face. The mirror showed a stuffed olive, round, sleek and sallow. And after the superior informed me I was being sent to Austin, Texas, I had put on five more pounds—up to two-fifteen—from funneling in tasteless food as if to staunch an internal wound. I didn't understand why he hadn't stationed me here in my hometown, which, terrible as it could be, was at least familiar.

The obvious alternative was for me to abandon the Order, but before leaving Italy I had vowed to postpone any decision until I'd been back in the States six months. I had envisioned a period of self-nurture in New York, examining my conscience, sorting through my options, checking the employment situation. But Texas? What could I do there? Mere mention of the place prevented me from thinking straight.

And yet, beset now by doubts about my doubts, I wasn't ready to call it quits and resign from the Paulists. Departures have always been painful for me, charged with a palpable sense of danger. My psychiatrist said this isn't unusual since all travel is a dream-symbol for death. But I began to wonder: if the idea of a four-hour flight to Texas was enough to unnerve me, what would it be like to leave the Church? Now, there was a journey that did indeed remind me of death. I thought of it all week as I made the rounds among relatives and friends, telling them I was about to go off again.

Because Lenny and his wife Rita hadn't bothered writing the whole time I was away, it surprised me yesterday when he telephoned the rectory in New York. He had heard I was headed for Texas and wanted to say he was sorry I was leaving. Although he sounded sincere, he had a longstanding habit of belittling me even as he expressed sympathy. "Better drop over here for dinner. You won't be getting any good grub where you're headed, partner."

Despite misgivings, I agreed to come, for Lenny was my only brother and a mystery I was determined to solve in the hope of understanding myself better. He was five years younger than I was, but had always acted older and treated me as his kid brother. The first time I saw him swing along the subway straps, smug and reckless as a monkey, I realized he'd soon outdistance me. A salesman, he had hustled encyclopedias, peddled Tupperware, bargained on cocoa bean futures, then made a fortune booking television time. "Dig it?" A playful poke to my ribs. Shooting back a shirt cuff, he would show his watch. "Time! It's free—but me, I'm selling it."

As I reached Riverside Drive and spotted the candy-striped canopy in front of Lenny's building, I wondered whether any trace of his enormous energy and earning power flowed in my veins. He and Rita owned a top-floor co-op where the living room was sunken, and their bedroom opened onto a balcony surrounded by wrought-iron railings. The kitchen was the color of avocados and mangoes, the bathroom had a bronze toilet. "Life's what you make it," Lenny liked to say. "You get out of it what you put into it."

But to me life seemed more like a slot machine. After you'd dropped your wad into it, twirling up lemons every time, Lenny would yank the handle once and hit the jackpot.

The glass door to the lobby was locked. When I rapped on it, a frosty-haired man in uniform lumbered over, pulling a ring of keys from under his brass-button coat.

"Yeah?"

"I'm here to see Mr. Amico."

"Oh, yeah." He let me in, locking up afterward. "The elevator's this way."

"I know. Thanks. I'll do it."

"No trouble." He got into the paneled box beside me.

"Top floor, please."

"Sure, sure. I'm friends with all the tenants. A fine fella, Mr. Amico. You're his brother, ain't you?"

I nodded as the door shut and the elevator lifted abruptly. I discovered myself concentrating on the Musak, that ubiquitous aural intrusion, the wallpaper of music. Once back in

America, my eyes and ears gorged omniverously on all manner of insipidness, while my mind tried to avoid more troublesome matters.

Suddenly gears ground and the elevator shuddered under my feet and lodged between floors twelve and fourteen. Shutting his eyes, the doorman dropped to one knee. "Bless me, Fadder, for I have sinned. It's been four years since my last confession."

"What is this?"

"In that time I been using rubbers two, three times a week. Add it up and that's a lot of mortal sins. But we got five kids, Fadder, and I can't afford any more."

"Get up," I said. "Go to church and confess."

One eye cracked open a centimeter, arching his bushy brow. "I'm on night duty. I sleep days."

"You haven't been on night duty four years. You must have free time."

"Not much. From month to month I might not run into a priest. But I know you're one. I seen you around here with a collar." He crawled closer to me.

"Don't you go to Mass?" I threw out the question like a scrap of meat to a mad dog as I backed into a corner.

"Like I say, I'm a busy man. But I try to be a good Catholic. Don't let me down, Fadder."

"I can't hear confessions in an elevator."

"In an emergency . . ."

"This isn't one. I'd like to help, but you'll have to go to a local priest. I'm not from this parish. I'm from . . . from Texas."

"Yeah, sure you are." Both eyes opened. "That's what's wrong with this world. Here I'm looking for spiritual guidance, and all you're worried about is legal loopholes. Don't you understand, I got four years' worth of rubbers on my conscience?"

"Say a good Act of Contrition and talk to your pastor tomorrow. Now, if you'll please get up, I'm late for dinner."

"Doesn't look to me like you've missed any meals lately." He stood up and stabbed a finger at the buttons. "What if I died during the night? You'd let me go to hell, wouldn't you? People do get killed in this city, you know."

Here it comes, I thought, the knife, the gun, the garrote. DERANGED DOORMAN SLAYS PRIEST IN ELEVATOR. But the door slid aside at the top floor and I darted out.

"Thanks for nothing," he said.

In spite of the air conditioning, I was sweating and the mustard-colored shirt stuck to my back. I felt I had narrowly escaped danger. But danger of what? Of the doorman? Or of doing my duty? It was as if I feared each sacrament I performed would add another day to my six-month sentence.

Before I had recovered, Lenny came out of his apartment. I started to speak, but he said, "Shhh," and quietly closed the door behind him. Stepping over to the interior staircase, he motioned for me to follow him onto the landing where it was fiercely hot and a garbage-scented wind whistled up from the ground floor. He clasped me to his chest. "How are you, buddy?"

"Not bad. And you?"

"*Così così.*" That exhausted his Italian. Though he claimed to have become "ethnically aware" in the last few years, he'd never learned the language. "I guess you heard Rita had a nervous breakdown."

"No! Nobody mentioned. You never wrote. Why didn't you say something on the phone?"

"What, and upset her? She was standing beside me, nursing the baby. That's right. She had a kid, too. A boy. The shrink says she's starting to recover from the breakdown, but she hasn't gotten over the baby yet and it's about to drive me bananas. I mean, okay, the kid helped cure her head, but what the hell cures a baby?"

"I wish you'd told me about this. If there's anything I—"

"Simple. Another baby. But who can afford it? Only deadbeats on welfare. Fatherhood's more expensive than owning a string of polo ponies."

Lenny's appearance troubled me deeply, and I put a hand on his shoulder in an attempt to pin down what was wrong. He wore an iridescent suit pressed to sharp edges, his silver tie resembled a sword, and his pointed shoes gleamed. But although highly polished as always, he seemed thin and brittle, a razor that had been stropped too often. "Sorry I wasn't around to lend you and Rita a hand. It must have been a tough time."

"You better believe it. But I didn't want to bother you in Rome. You had your own troubles."

News of Rita's breakdown and their baby somehow rattled me more than his usual insults and arrogance might have. "Look, why don't we postpone this until Rita's back on her feet?"

"No, she's dying to talk to you. And you can't leave without seeing the kid."

"She must be busy with the baby. I don't like to put her to extra trouble."

"I told you, no trouble. It's good for her to be busy. Keeps her mind occupied." Lenny's dark gaze wavered. "You see, she's still not in tiptop shape. I thought maybe since you've been, you know, through the same thing, you could give her advice and encouragement."

"I want to help, but I don't know whether it was the same thing. I'm not a psychiatrist."

"But you're a priest."

This caused me a long pause. I had never heard Lenny emphasize that fact except in jokes. "The breakdown," I said, "how did it happen? Rita always seemed so strong-willed."

"Oh, Christ," he sighed, "who knows? It began with her bitching about not having anything to believe in. I told her it was just a phase, but she said she didn't even want to get out of bed in the morning. A friend of ours suggested a baby. So we did that, and then she had too much to believe in. Breast-feeding, baths, burping, diapers. Now she's complaining she doesn't have any time to be committed. I'm telling you, Tony, I'm about to *have* her committed. You gotta talk to her."

"I don't think she'll take my word."

"Sure she will. She respects you. We both do. Let's go in before she gets worried." As we left the landing, Lenny flung an arm around my shoulder. "One more thing. Notice the kid. Make a big fuss over him. Rita's very touchy about that."

"Of course. I can't wait to meet the little guy."

The instant I entered the apartment, I saw why I'd been warned. Rita stood at the dining table—a slab of glass on a trestle of tubular chrome—working at what looked to be a lump of wriggling dough. The baby was plump and blanched, with Lenny's dark eyes glowering under Rita's auburn brows. Maybe Lenny had feared I'd find him ugly. But I must have inherited a portion of my mother's instincts, for I had always loved babies.

Rita herself had lost weight and color and shape, and with her dress pulled down off one shoulder, the left cup of her brassiere flapping loose, she looked like a waif in hand-me-down clothes. Her small breast was red, raw, and almost all nipple.

I came close and kissed the cheek she offered. "You look wonderful. And the baby, he's beautiful."

"Thanks, Tony. But I don't deserve any compliments. It's what women are made for. I wish I'd had one sooner," she said with a glare at Lenny, "but we were saving for stock options." She pulled back from me and powdered the baby's bottom.

After a moment's silence, I said, "Well, I'm off to Texas tomorrow."

"You're going to roast your ass off," Lenny said.

"They tell me it's a dry heat."

"Yeah, sure. Texas, it's the dry heaves."

"You should stay here and have a baby." Rita continued her diapering.

"That might be a bit of a problem, don't you think?" I asked.

"Let nature take care of the problems. I don't know about men, but women have these things inside them begging to be satisfied."

"I believe men's insides are a little different."

"Okay, smart-ass. You know what she means." Lenny leaped to her defense. "You should settle down, find a job, get married, have a family."

"Don't be stupid." I acted insulted, just as I did whenever anyone suggested the solution I had entertained.

"Stupid, hell! Have you heard about the priests who taught us in high school? After all their bullshit about keeping your pecker in your pants, half of them went A.W.O.L. Marriage is breaking up that old gang of yours. Father Damien has three kids."

"That's his business. It's between him and his confessor."

"Confessor! Fat chance you'd find him in church. He owns a head shop in the Village. They're all into one weird trip or another. The whole scene is so typical of the Catholic Church, always about twenty years behind the times. I mean, for Chrissake, just when marriage is losing popularity with lay people, it's catching on with the clergy!"

"I think I'd better go," I said.

"Don't be touchy. We're just joking. Right, Rita?" He held me by the arm. "Come here and have a look at the equipment on this kid. You believe the size of it?" He pointed to the stubby Vienna sausage of the baby's sex. "Remember when I was little how people said I'd have to grow up into my nose? This kid, it'll take him twenty years to grow into that peperoni."

"Lenny's as bad as those priests." Rita finished pinning the diaper, then lifted the baby, whose mouth was searching for her nipple. "His concept of sex is so limited, so adolescent."

"She had her consciousness raised," Lenny said, leading the way down into the living room. He made it sound like bridgework or plastic surgery. "We did the natural childbirth number. You know, the Lamaze Method. I was right there in the delivery room, helping her push and taking pictures. We'll show you the slides later."

"I'd love to see them." The three of us sat down on a couch whose upholstery felt cold and uncomfortable as chicken wire. "What's his name?" I asked.

"Rolf," said Rita, as the baby fastened himself ferociously to her breast.

"Come again?"

"Rolf," Lenny repeated gutturally.

"It's German," Rita said. "We named him after my masseur. A super fellow. For the first time in months I can sleep after a rubdown."

"And that's what you baptized him?"

Rita smiled and looked at Lenny. "Tony, don't tell me you still believe in all those sad old lies. I can't imagine after being on your own in Rome for a year you could still be the same. Lenny bet me it wouldn't change you, but I thought he was joking."

"Joking? What's so funny? Look, I'm feeling much better. I got a good rest and had a chance to think things over. But my problems didn't have anything to do with religion."

"Sure they did," Lenny said. "They had to."

"Well, maybe that was part of it, but the point is—"

"The point is," said Lenny, "no one's a Catholic any more. Nobody believes it does a damn bit of good to sprinkle water on a baby's head."

"Wait a minute. I do." I forced some conviction into my voice as I studied Rolf's head, which, under its reddish fuzz, appeared papery, easily crushed. "What if he died without being baptized?"

"What are you trying to do," Lenny asked, "scare us back into the faith? I refuse to let fear rule my life."

"There's so much more to believe in," Rita said, plucking at the right cup of her bra. The Velcro gave way with an adhesive rip, and she switched Rolf to the other breast. "I really feel sorry for you, Tony. You need a woman."

Later, when Lenny and I went out on the terrace overlooking the dark scar of the river and sizzled steaks on the charcoal grill, a smell like incense clung to our clothing and insinuated itself into the apartment. "For Chrissake, I thought you were on my side," he hissed, stabbing a fork at the meat. "You see how she is. You want to knock her over the edge? I need your help, Tony, not a lot of crap from the Baltimore Catechism. Lay off religion. It sends Rita through the roof."

"I don't mean to upset her."

"But that's what you're doing. I said encourage her. Help her. Don't lay another load on her."

"I can't deny my beliefs."

"Okay, we understand your position, but you gotta make allowances for our agnosticism. It's not so much I don't believe in God. He just doesn't matter. I mean like what's sin, any more? All I ever had to confess was whacking off or copping a few cheap feels. Now that I'm married, how can I commit a sin? I get grace for doing it, don't I? And without sin, what's the use of religion?"

"I hope you're kidding, Lenny. That's a retarded notion of Church theology."

"Theology, pee-ology. Every time you turn around, they switch the rules to suit the season." He flipped the steak, and the hive of briquettes buzzed. "You take meat. What happened to those guys in the old days who ate it on Friday? They went to hell, right? Well, what I'm interested in is how things worked out after they changed the rule. Did those guys get time off for good behavior or a pardon or amnesty or what?"

"You may think you're funny, but you're making a fool of yourself. There's a lot more to Catholicism than the laws of fast and abstinence."

"Yeah, what? And how does it fit in with what I see down there?" He jabbed the twin-tined fork over the railing. "You been on the streets lately? It looks like *Zoo Parade.*"

"Maybe you should work to change things for the better. You could give good example and bear witness to the—"

Lenny blew a reedy snort through his nostrils. "Not me, brother. I'm no witness. I didn't see a thing, Mr. Policeman. So put away your notebook. I ain't going to testify."

We brought the platter of steaks into the dining room, sat at the table and paused before serving ourselves, gazing through the glass top at our legs which looked as though they were in water up to the thighs, our bones bending with the tide. Perhaps they thought I was saying grace to myself.

Once we were eating, the silence bothered me almost as much as Lenny's banter had. So I made a few neutral remarks, avoiding all abstractions and the slightest suggestion of what they might have referred to as "philosophical discussion."

It's funny about philosophy. Though laying no claims as a savant myself, I've learned the hard way that most people know little about it except that they don't like it. On the rare occasion when anyone does volunteer to discourse on his "philosophy," he usually goes on to offer stock tips or advise you to rotate your tires every ten thousand miles.

"Jesus," groaned Rita, "I'm so depressed, and it's all because of you, Tony, and this business about God."

"How are your breasts?" asked Lenny.

She cupped one in either hand. "Hard and sore. I wish I hadn't eaten the meat. Mine was burnt. I heard on a talk show where you can catch cancer from too much charcoal. Would Rolf be affected through my milk?"

I gnawed the last cinder of my own steak, anxious to finish eating and be on my way. Yet after dessert, after Lenny's mordant needling and Rita's black mood, they wouldn't hear of letting me cut short our last evening together. Talking of the tiring, terrifying ride I would have to risk on the subway, dismissing my murmur about taxis, they insisted I spend the night—and I'll admit it, in spite of everything I appreciated the welcome. It was late, the dinner had left me lethargic, and I dreaded returning to the rectory to sleep alone in the guest room surrounded by my half-packed suitcases. So I said I'd stay and I hoped the snifters of Grand Marnier would mellow them, and that finally we'd talk about old times, old friends, the family.

But Rita snuffed out the candles with her fingers, and they began to get ready for bed. Lenny had a staff meeting first thing in the morning; she would have to wake before dawn to feed the baby. They unfolded the living room couch like a portfolio, spread a rubberized mat over the mattress and covered it with a contour sheet. Then, as they climbed toward their balcony bedroom, Rita called breezily over her shoulder, "Good night, Tony. Be sure to say your prayers."

Stripping to my underwear, I knelt in the darkness next to the sofa, shivering in a room which because of its gleaming alloys and synthetic fibers felt unnaturally cool. I tried to concentrate on praying—on any prayer—but nothing worked. I wondered what it would be like to have a woman, a wife, beside me tonight. Not simply for sex or the sort of love I had listened to my parishioners describe in confession with a mixture of contrition and pride, but someone to relieve the loneliness, to lie awake with me talking about tomorrow and the move to Texas and what kind of city Austin would be.

Yet what woman would have me? I glanced at my belly and cursed myself for overeating. How hideous I must have been even in the eyes of the Lord. There were whiskey priests and womanizers, haters, homosexuals and charlatans, but their offenses were no worse than my weakness for second and third helpings, my craving not for a particular taste or texture, but for fullness, a false sense of completion. Still, I knelt until my knees were numb and I was no longer shivering.

In the nursery the baby whined once, then was quiet. Poor little Rolf, I thought.

I leaned my head into my hands, covering my eyes, but then made myself stand up. Barefoot, I padded into the bathroom, drew a glass of water, and edged into the nursery where Rolf was bundled in a bassinet. Without taking more time to reflect, I tilted the glass, spilling a few drops on his forehead and whispering, "I baptize thee in the name of the Father and of the Son and of the Holy Spirit."

As water ran in rivulets down both sides of his nose, he came awake and cried. "Shhh," I said softly, drying his cheeks with the blanket. But when he began to howl, I started shivering again and for an insane instant I was tempted to clamp a hand over his mouth. Heading for the door, I heard footsteps in the hall, unhurried and unshod.

Rita shuffled in and flicked on a lamp. She didn't seem surprised to find me standing there in my underwear. Bare-breasted, pinpoints of white speckling her nipples, she stifled a yawn and smiled. "You look like a big Easter rabbit in that outfit."

"I didn't bring my pajamas."

"Finished yet?"

"I was getting a drink"—I held up the glass—"when I heard the baby crying. I thought I'd better check on him."

"Oh, Tony, you don't have to lie. I know you baptized him.

Lenny bet me you would. Not that it matters much one way or the other."

The glass slipped from my hand and shattered. Staggering, I came down on a jagged sliver. I didn't cry out, but Rolf howled louder and Rita yelled for Lenny to bring the Band-Aids.

I

Rain and wind lashed the Braniff 727, and the wing on my side looked as trembling and insubstantial as an insect's. The fusilage, painted brilliant orange, reminded me of the throat lozenges I used to suck on as a boy. Somehow that didn't bolster my confidence. When we took off from grimy, overcast Newark, I had murmured an almost audible Act of Contrition, and once we were airborne I continued to pray, shamefully aware that I was seldom so fervent as when I flew.

A stewardess with a fixed grin strolled the aisle, offering magazines. I asked for *Newsweek, Time, Fortune* and *Holiday,* hoping to read and forget my fear, but I wound up hugging them to my stomach. Inside me some vital organ seemed to have swung free from its mooring, and I kept a paper bag standing ready between my knees. At Lenny and Rita's I had washed down a huge breakfast with four cups of coffee. Now a needling disquiet commenced in my descending bowel, yet I didn't dare get up and walk to the men's room for fear the slightest movement might bring on a fit of vomiting.

Having studied the statistics, I knew I was safer in the air than in an average household kitchen, and though that didn't help much at the moment, it did perhaps explain why I'd been so jittery this morning in Lenny and Rita's kitchen. Sitting with them at the breakfast bar had been like squirming on the anxious bench. Neither of them had mentioned last night; neither had asked me to explain why I baptized Rolf—which only confirmed my suspicion that they had set me up. But I didn't need them to impress upon me the enormity of my actions. Now Rolf was a Catholic whether he wanted to be or not, and I couldn't imagine what the world would be like when he first felt that barbed hook buried in his soul.

Actually, I found it difficult to say what the world was like today, and looking around did little to enlighten me. The other passengers, sipping cocktails from styrene plastic glasses, wore tight leather trousers, fringed suede jackets, safari outfits, brass pendants and legionnaire sandals, while I sat among them in my dark suit and clerical collar like a chunk of negative space, what the scientists call a black hole.

Yet a lovely girl in appliquéed jeans was at least aware of my existence. Taking a paperback from her purse, she showed me the cover of *The Exorcist.* "Hey, Father, ever get into one of these?"

"Lately I haven't had time to do much reading. Is it good?"

"I mean did you ever have any dealings with devils? You know, casting them out and stuff?"

"No, most of my work is with humans."

Not bothering to conceal her disappointment, she soon turned from me to the book. Like a lot of priests, I was baffled by this craze for the occult, especially for demonology. Although not many people admitted to a belief in God, everybody seemed sure about Satan.

In Washington, the trappers and Indians, white hunters and legionnaires got off the plane, and what appeared to be a convention of golf pros climbed aboard. Jaunty and loud, these men sported gaudy double-knit outfits, wide white belts, and white turtle-skin shoes with tassels. Plastic badges had been pinned to their lapels, certifying them as members of the Centex Oculists Association. It used to be you knew you were in the South when you spotted a Clabber Girl sign or a Bull Durham billboard. Now, according to Lenny, you couldn't be sure you had arrived until you saw the first covey of men in bright leisure suits.

One fellow in a powder-blue jacket squeezed by me, crumpling the vomit bag, and flopped where the girl had been. His badge said, HI! I'M CORKY. " 'Scuse me, Reverend. You finished this one?" He lifted *Fortune* from my lap, an issue with Ralph Nader on the cover, and flicked his fingernail against Nader's nose. "Know what I'd like? I'd for once like to hear this guy shut up."

What he heard was me shut up for the duration of the flight. Oh God, I thought, maybe it's better if the plane does go down. What purpose could I serve in Texas? I doubted I could communicate with the group that had just gotten off or with the one that had gotten on. At best, I could conceive of myself as a keeper, not a defender, of the faith—a caretaker, someone who stood around patiently like those men in museums watching over dusty antiques and bones. My last hope seemed to be that religious belief would make a comeback like nostalgia for the 50's or platform shoes and padded shoulders.

It was raining in Texas, too, and over Austin the airplane dropped turbulently through thunder, sheets of lightning and great bolsters of clouds. I didn't need to fasten my seat belt. I had never loosened it, and now it had the effect of forcing my stomach toward my throat. Shutting my eyes, I crushed the bag between my knees, swallowed, and tasted bile. When the wheels smacked down on the runway, I relaxed for the first time in four hours, and Corky, in a hurry, clambered over me.

While other passengers sprinted through the downpour, I walked slowly, with my head thrown back to catch the cool drops on my cheeks. Reaching the chain link fence at the edge of the asphalt, I slumped against it and breathed deep to let the fresh air restore me. Rain beat at my head and bare neck, trickled down my arms and puddled at my elbows. Though my collar had lost starch, it still felt like a noose, and I was about to unbutton it when someone touched my shoulder.

"Father Amico?"

"Yes." I glanced up at a tall white fellow with a bushy, imitation Afro haircut, muttonchop sideburns and wire-rim glasses. The embroidery on his Mexican peasant's blouse bled purple dye.

"I'm Larry Sparks. Welcome to Austin."

He held out his hand, and as we stood in the rain solemnly shaking, I noticed over his shoulder that a crowd at the waiting room window was peering at us through clouds of condensation. Immediately, I realized my mistake. I shouldn't have let anyone from St. Austin's see me falter. I was afraid the parishioners and other priests might treat me with kindness yet consider me a trooper who had broken in battle. I'd have to be on guard or they'd assume I'd gone around the bend again.

"Glad to meet you, Larry. Just catching my breath. We had a bumpy flight."

"Sorry to hear that. The car's around front, Father Amico."

"Call me Tony. Nice-looking shirt there." I took Larry's arm and led him toward the terminal, striving for an impression of control. "Are you a priest?" I asked, unable to guess from his hair, Levis and scuffed *huaraches*, and unwilling to risk more mistakes.

"Yes, of course. How were things in Rome?"

"Very, very . . ." What were the right words? "Peaceful and productive."

As my nausea subsided and we moved in out of the rain, I remembered how badly I had to go to the bathroom. Larry volunteered to collect my luggage while I hurried off to the men's room, and although I couldn't have been gone more than a few minutes, he was waiting for me just outside the lavatory. We collided as I came through the door.

"Are you okay?" he asked, suspicious or solicitous—I couldn't say which.

"Sure. All set."

The storm had broken and burly clouds stampeded east, leaving behind a sinking sun and a sky inlaid with the enameled color one sees in New York on smoggy evenings. From the airport we drove west in a purple Pontiac GTO, the same shade as the stain on Larry's shirt. The car had a broad white racing stripe, gumball tires, Naugahyde bucket seats, a tachometer and a four-speed floor shift which was as much a mystery to Fr. Sparks as it would have been to me. At stoplights and corners, he down-shifted before applying the brakes but often forgot the clutch, and the gearbox clattered in protest.

"Isn't this the worst car you've ever seen? I'm almost embarrassed to drive it," Larry said. "But somebody donated it to the parish, and it does come in handy. I can get anywhere almost as fast as an ambulance or the police, and it's brought me closer to certain kids in the community."

"Is that so?"

"Ed Haskins—he owns a used-car lot out on Interregional—let us have a nice Vega for you. Wait till you see it. It's sort of lemon-drop yellow."

"I don't drive."

"You're kidding." The Pontiac bucked and snorted as Larry let up on the gas.

"No. I always lived in New York until this last year. I never learned."

"Oh Lord, they're not going to be happy to hear this. You won't be able to pitch in on the home and hospital visits. It's bound to cut down on our mobility."

"I'll walk. Or use buses and cabs."

He shook his frizzy head. "No, Tony, this is big country. We've got a lot of territory to cover. You'll have to get a license."

I nodded, but knew I wouldn't. They'd have to accept me as I was or—hope seized me—send me back to New York.

Contrary to Larry's claim, Texas didn't look like Big Country or any more like the west than Weehawken, New Jersey. True, a few palms and cactus plants struggled for survival on the median strip, but every other inch of the asphalt we sped over was lined by discount drugstores, cut-rate gas stations, barbecue pits, fortune tellers, wig outlets, warehouses, vast parking lots and a dizzying assortment of fast-food chains. Nothing unusual about that. As American as the Golden Arches. What had I expected, adobe huts and cattle on the open range? Yet somehow the familiar scene didn't improve my spirits.

As we waited for a red light at a wide two-tier highway, soggy air, growing warmer, washed through the car. Where was the dry heat? Larry pressed a button to raise the windows, then crossed Interstate 35, and I spotted the Texas Tower and a stonehenge of tall, stark buildings done in what Larry called "a Mediterranean motif." Which meant red tile roofs. My eye was attracted to an immense football stadium, the omphalos of the University of Texas campus, but Larry pointed right. "Over there's the LBJ Library. People say if you like Mussolini's Rome, you'll love it."

I smiled, although the white bunker of a building resembled no Italian monument I had seen, and it seemed more likely to contain prisoners than books. Its façade was webbed with scaffolding. "When do they expect to have it completed?"

"Oh, it's been finished for years. Started falling apart right after they opened it. They're putting a new face on it."

Swinging away from the University, he followed a cross

street where other forbidding stone structures alternated with rubble-strewn lots overrun by weeds. Each building with its slabs of concrete and slotlike windows looked as if it had been designed with an eye to easy defense. Very few people were on the sidewalks.

"How far are we from town?"

Larry squinted at me through his wire-rim spectacles. "This is the town."

"This? Here?"

"Well, more or less." But he shot a quick look around, as if unsure. "There aren't many people around in August, so it looks a little deserted," he admitted. "We're between the summer session and the fall semester. But wait till next month." Larry took a right onto a street which was brightly lit and broad, yet again virtually empty. "This is Guadelupe. The students call it The Drag. And that's the plant over there."

St. Austin's bore the most rudimentary resemblance to a church, and could have been a false front from a movie set. The building had apparently been white before smoke or smog had discolored the concrete block walls. Making a U-turn, Larry stopped in front of the rectory, not far from a clump of red oleanders next to the entrance. If it hadn't been for that lovely bush, I doubt I could have brought myself to climb out and unload the baggage.

The temperature was still rising, but I had begun to perspire as much from nerves as from the heat. Larry must have noticed my fidgety mood. He kept up a constant stream of chatter about the liberal city government and the energetic parish and the mild winters and good country music as we stacked my black suitcases on the sidewalk. Then he paused and said, "To be honest, Tony, Texas takes some getting used to. It was months before I felt at home. But you'll like it here if you let yourself."

"I'm going to try," I said, drawing a breath. "It smells like they have dinner waiting for us."

"No, they eat early. It's always like that on The Drag because . . ."

His voice trailed off as he motioned in either direction to an all but unbroken row of restaurants, snack bars, fried-chicken stands and pizza parlors, each one with an exhaust fan funneling out the odor of French-fried everything.

Larry picked up two suitcases. "What do you say we go in and meet the others?"

The rectory was dim and air-conditioned, and we bumped the luggage through the reception area, past the switchboard, the religious pamphlets and holy pictures, and down an unlit corridor at the end of which I heard loud voices. Larry stopped and set the suitcases on the floor.

"Excuse me, fellows. Father Amico's here."

From behind him I gazed into a room which was impenetrably dark except for the penumbra of a TV screen. What had sounded like an argument proved to be an exhibition game between the Cowboys and the Rams: *Staubach crunches off left tackle for two and the Cowboys will put the ball into play from* . . . Someone pried himself out of a chair; I recognized the sound of rayon pants peeling away from Leatherette upholstery. A fluorescent bulb in the ceiling flickered, then flashed on with dazzling force as half a dozen men heaved themselves to their feet, blinking, unsteady. The light raised a painful glare from the tile floor and imitation oak paneling.

A baldheaded man stepped forward, grinning.

"Father Ryan, this is Father Amico," Larry said. "Tony, this is the pastor."

"Please, call me Tom."

"Tony here. Sorry to interrupt the game."

"No trouble. Dallas is doing fine." Fr. Ryan sneaked a sidelong glance at the screen. "Are you a fan?"

On this subject I had learned it served no purpose to speak the truth. "Sort of."

"Great, you're in the right place. We're on the cable and

pick up all the games from Houston and Dallas. And there's the U.T. team. They always wind up in the Top Ten and the Cotton Bowl and . . . Why don't you come on in and let me introduce you to the gang?"

Though they all wore civilian clothes, they seemed to come from opposing camps. The younger ones were dressed in faded jeans, desert boots, work shirts, long hair, sideburns and beards. But even out of the habit the older priests looked liturgically correct in their drab baggy trousers, plain blue or white shirts and shiny black shoes, the kind you see for sale in Navy surplus stores. I couldn't help recalling the chasm between the double-knit crowd and the theatrical costumers on the airplane, and I wondered whether it was the same right here in the rectory and where my age and attitude would put me. Between the two factions, catching flak from both directions? Or out of it altogether?

At a roar all eyes swung around to the TV set. Dallas had hurtled close to the goal line, and that gave us a good excuse not to stare at one another.

"I bet you're tired," Fr. Ryan said while the Cowboys huddled. "And hungry. Have you eaten?"

"A big breakfast, then a snack on the plane. But I *am* tired. The time change, I guess. I'm still not right after that return flight from Rome."

Fr. Ryan's expression changed. "Of course. Larry'll show you your room. It's a bit bare, but we decided it'd be better to let you furnish it to suit yourself. Tomorrow you can go over to the Redemption Center and pick up whatever you need."

"The Redemption Center?"

"For Green Stamps. You know, the kind you save and trade in. We've got hundreds of books. Folks give them to us all the time. You'll find these Texans are very friendly, generous people, Tony. And the Redemption Center has everything you could want. Take the station wagon and—"

"He doesn't drive," Larry said.

"What?" Fr. Ryan's forehead, extraordinarily high because of his baldness, showed a three-inch ladder of furrows. "Impossible. Somebody would have told me."

"No one asked," I said. "I'm sorry."

"No problem. You'll just have to learn. Someone'll teach you." He nodded to the others as they watched Dallas dive in for a score. "We already have a car for you. Ed Haskins donated a little Vega."

"So Larry said."

"Why don't you get a good night's sleep?" the pastor said. "See you in the morning."

"Nice to have met you."

"Good night, Father," came a chorus of voices, a faint echo of the crowd as the extra point was kicked.

Houses and rooms, some people say, have their own personalities. If so, I'd have to describe the character of my quarters at St. Austin's as catatonic. Or perhaps that more accurately describes me the first time I entered that cubbyhole which was painted a sickly green and which contained a bed not much bigger than a cot, a crucifix on the wall, a gun-metal grey chest of drawers and a table lamp stranded in the middle of the floor.

"Father Ryan's right," Larry reassured me as he set my suitcases in a corner. "You really can get everything you need at the Redemption Center."

"That's good to know. Thanks for your help."

"Don't mention it. See you tomorrow, Tony." He stopped at the door and added, "We're all glad you're going to be with us." Then he was gone.

I sagged onto the bed and checked my watch. It was eight-thirty. Nine-thirty in New York. And in Rome . . . My mind was too fogged to figure that out, yet even now I could re-create the pleasing rituals of my life there—a morning cappuccino in a *caffe* near the monastery, afternoons spent prowling the Forum or the Palatine Hill, solitary evening walks when the city was turning terra cotta.

The memories made me feel as exhausted as I had claimed to be and more depressed than ever. I couldn't bear the idea of unpacking. Tomorrow was soon enough. Too soon.

Six months, I thought, prying off one shoe with the toe of the other. Not bothering to bend over and untie the laces, I slipped off the other shoe and flexed my feet. The soles stung. It would be a long time before I recovered from last night, and meanwhile I was anxious to withdraw like a turtle into its shell, taking no chances. Better to remain silent and absolutely still so the months would slide by like dreamless sleep.

I rechecked my watch. Five minutes wasted.

II

Although slow in coming, a riptide of sleep swirled around me at last and wrenched me under for ten hours. Presumably I dreamed. My psychiatrists swore everybody did, and during our sessions they expected me to recount broad-screen Technicolor extravaganzas, while when I remembered anything at all—which wasn't often—it was more like a home movie, grey, flickering, grainy and run at the wrong speed.

I woke, dressed swiftly and went down to say Mass. Six women were scattered about the church, shriveled and black-shawled like their counterparts in Italy. Chicanas, Larry Sparks informed me. Then after breakfast Fr. Ryan handed me dozens of Green Stamp books and said that David Pernoski, a deacon ten months from ordination, would drive me in the parish station wagon to the Redemption Center.

An affable boy with a sparse cinnamon-colored beard, David had an accent I couldn't place until I recalled a conversation I'd once had with a cashier at O'Hare Airport. When I went to pay, the woman had asked, "Will that be cherge or kesh, Father?" That's how David Pernoski spoke. Answering in the affirmative, he invariably said, "Fer shir." He was from Wilmette, Illinois, and confessed that at first the idea of moving to Texas had appalled him. But Austin, he had found, was a fine town, clean, friendly, and a terrific place to raise children.

Nodding, I agreed. Or, that is, I granted notional assent to the possibility of his opinion. Although I reserved final judgment, I wanted to be fair and open to everything. Certainly open to David, who revealed that he had been a member of the Roamin' Collars, a Paulist folk-singing group, with which he had traveled from parish to parish, taking stock of the Order. Though not yet a priest, he could have been a bishop. He displayed admirable energy and enthusiasm and an unswerving desire to modernize the Church and pull the Paulist community up by its sandal straps. He himself wore clunky shoes with soles higher at the toes than at the heels. It looked like he had put them on backward.

"We're the Missionaries to Main Street, right?" he asked as we drove up The Drag.

"Right," I said, savoring the fried bread crumb aroma.

"And the Paulists are dedicated to working in cities, on the streets, with the people, right?"

"Yes."

"Well, what worries me is how far we're falling behind the competition. The Trinitarians got a big jump on us. Have you heard what this Father Joseph Lupo up in Maryland's been doing?"

"No. Most rumors never reached Rome."

"You must have read about it. It was in all the papers. Father Lupo took out an ad for vocations in *Playboy.*"

"I don't subscribe."

"Neither do I, but a lot of young people read it, and the response to Lupo's ad was fantastic. He received hundreds of letters."

"All from fellows wanting to become priests?"

"No, a lot of them probably weren't Catholics and some of them had to have been crazy. You know, your average crackpot correspondent. But the crucial point is, people have become aware of the Church and what it's doing."

"What is it doing?" I asked, troubled despite my best intentions.

David combed his fingers through his whiskers and eyed me as if to ask, Aren't you listening? We were on the Expressway, I-35, and I would have preferred that he watch where he was headed, but he went on talking and driving heedlessly. "Well, for one thing, it's advertising in *Playboy.* That's a breakthrough. And it's coming out of its cocoon after centuries. It's showing more pizzazz and involving itself with what's happening. That's the name of the game these days.

"You take this Father Lupo. He didn't sit back on his aspirations. He followed up that first ad with a bigger one in *Rolling Stone.* He's determined to meet people on their own ground and speak to their needs. That's what it's all about, isn't it? If we hope to hit folks where they live, we have to know where they live."

"Maybe they're living at the Playboy Mansion."

His high seriousness unshakable, David didn't laugh. " 'My father's house has many mansions.' Every mission is a mixed bag today, Tony. Seems to me it's our duty to examine the secular and show how it's already sacred in some ways. It depends mostly on how you look at it. I'm sure there are souls out there"—his expansive gestures appeared to encompass the shopping centers, gas stations and construction sites we were passing—"who are yearning for us. We just have to find the way to reach them."

"Maybe you're right," I murmured, although I'd seldom had an inkling that anyone, except dying people, yearned for me and my help. "It's certainly something to consider. Is this the Redemption Center?"

"Fer shir." Coasting across the lot, David drew close to a yellow brick building with suites of furniture in the front window. Then, swiveling around in the seat, he fixed me with earnest eyes. "Look, Tony, if I proposed that the Paulists buy an ad in, let's say, *Penthouse* or *Oui*, could I count on your support?"

"I'll have to think that over," I said, still striving to be open and agreeable.

"That's all I ask."

We got out of the car and raced through the afternoon heat as though through a rainstorm. Fr. Ryan—and Larry Sparks, in repeating the pastor's words—had been absolutely right, I decided as I picked up a catalog and pushed through a turnstile into the display area. Here in the Redemption Center I could find everything I needed, and I got giddy with relief when I saw that I could shove my troubles out of mind and concentrate on shiny new objects. Perhaps Lenny and Rita had discovered this secret to happiness ages ago.

Lugging stacks of Green Stamps, I strolled from one showcase to another, stunned by the plentitude and by the notion that nothing here cost money. It could all be had for books—a neat psychological ploy, since they constituted the lowest valued commodity in our culture.

For a while I wandered amid the camping and recreational equipment, where a bearded mannequin lay in a loden green pup tent, snug in a down-filled sleeping bag, reading a book by a cheerful red Coleman lantern. Nearby rested a cast-iron hibachi to cook on, a two-gallon thermos to drink from, and a sturdy ice chest for storing food. I had stepped close to check how many books the entire campsite cost when David Pernoski nudged my elbow.

"Uh . . . Tony, the furniture's down this way."

"Yes, of course. Just looking for Christmas ideas."

Afraid the boy had been warned to watch for signs of instability, I shunted aside my daydreams of pup tents and a womb away from home, and moved with grave purpose among the household goods. Quickly I chose a desk which had brushed-chrome legs and a pecan Permaneer finish. It looked murderously efficient and ineffably cheap. Nobody could complain about it or the matching bookshelf.

The foam-filled black vinyl swivel chair I selected next might have struck somebody as an extravagance at eighteen and three-quarters books, but I believed it could do double duty at the desk and as an easy chair. Still, I decided I'd better compensate by forgoing a throw rug, all knickknacks, and the spearlike pole lamp that particularly appealed to me.

For the lamp I already had I needed a table and debated between beauty and frugality. I liked what the catalog described as "a Mersman Mediterranean Style Poe Table with an oak wood finish and a slate-like hi-pressure laminated plastic top," but to save the parish nineteen books I settled for the "Gotham parsons table with a wet-look finish of high impact polymer."

"Okay, David, if you'll lend me a hand . . ." Dropping the stamps onto the seat of the swivel chair, I dried my palms on my hips and got a good grip on one end.

"Uh, Tony, they take care of that. This is just a display."

"They?"

"The people in the storeroom." He signaled vaguely. "You, uh, tell them the serial numbers up at the cash register. They collect the books and have somebody carry the stuff around front."

"Yes. That makes sense."

Waiting for the warehouse workers, we stayed in the station wagon with the engine running and the air conditioner set on Hi-Cool. That helped me very little. I felt warm, frazzled and guilty after my orgy of commerce, and not even a pup tent or placenta-like sleeping bag could have protected me from a sudden sense of desolation—or from the ebullient naïveté of David Pernoski.

Concerning matrimony, he said, he understood how it might appeal to some men but it could never be his calling. I refused to admit my true thoughts and mumbled something about the current confusion over vocations. When he expressed the opinion that priests who left the Church to marry had chosen an easy way out, I kept quiet. It didn't strike me as such an easy exit, and I was reminded of that Japanese soldier who after thirty years in the Philippine jungles had been caught and finally convinced World War II was over. His captors believed they were doing him a favor, but the soldier had cried out in anguish when he learned he had wasted his life. That instant of recognition may well have been as painful as all those decades of living in caves and eating roots and insects. Sometimes it seemed to require more courage to surrender and face the truth.

Back at the rectory, David and a few priests helped me drag the huge cardboard boxes upstairs and stack them beside my suitcases. These acquisitions did transform the atmosphere of the room—from that of a monastic cell to a mortuary.

"Guess I'd better get to work," I said. "Thanks, fellas."

"Want a hand?" David asked. "Some of the furniture you might have to put together."

"No, don't bother. I need the exercise." Smiling, I patted my stomach.

When they left, I lifted the lamp off the floor and placed it on the box containing the Parsons table. Then, perching on the edge of the bed, I struggled to get my thoughts straight. The swivel chair would have been more comfortable, but I feared that once I unpacked the furniture it would mean I had moved in for good, and I wasn't willing to face that.

That evening at dinner I regarded my fellow priests in much the same fashion as I did the boxes and baggage in my room. It may sound uncharitable, but I sensed that once I invited them to open up about themselves, I would have arrived officially and be beyond recall. I kept my eyes on my plate and my mouth shut or stuffed with food.

"Are you satisfied with your furniture?" Fr. Ryan asked.

"It's fine."

"And that room? No one's lived in it for a while, and I realize it's awfully small."

"I haven't finished unpacking."

"Of course. Take your time. Get settled, get used to things," he said. "I think we ought to put Tony on hospital duty at first. Don't you, Father Doyle?"

"Yes, that'll give him a chance to get acquainted. A lot of the hospitals are within walking distance. It'll be good duty while you're learning to drive."

"Thank you, Father."

"Don't mention it. You see much of Austin this afternoon?" Fr. Doyle asked. He had a full head of hair—yellowish white—but was older than Fr. Ryan. He was far older, in fact, than anyone at St. Austin's, and with false teeth too large for his sunken face he had a ferocious smile.

"Just on the road to and from the Redemption Center."

"Quite a change after Rome, I bet. But you'll find it a friendly city. No frills, no pretentions, just plain good folks. I've been here twenty years and like it more every day."

"I'm sure I'll . . . I'll see it all before long." I shoveled in a forkful of mashed potatoes.

"You know, Tony, Texans look on Austin as a kind of Mecca. Maybe it's the hills."

"The hills?"

"Yes, west of here there're hills. Big, beautiful ones. Folks travel from all over to see them. David, why don't you drive him out to our hills?"

"Fer shir, Father."

"And take him through some of the nice neighborhoods.

They'll show you what a fine place this is to raise a family."

Mouth stuffed with more mashed potatoes, I couldn't ask, Why? Why remind me what a marvelous place Austin was to raise kids? Maybe they were hinting I was washed up as a priest and might as well be fruitful and multiply. Or was there simply nothing else to say about the city?

During the days that I trudged from hospital to hospital visiting sick parishioners, I discovered a great deal more to say about Austin. The problem was how to express it. Since I felt so abstracted from my surroundings, I attempted to imagine how an Italian tourist might react.

Ma fa caldo. The first day I wore my black suit like a penance, but abandoned it thereafter for loose-fitting, short-sleeved shirts. Soon my face and arms were as dark as a Sicilian fisherman's. In the afternoon, heat flowed palpably down The Drag like lava through the streets of Pompeii. Shimmering with mirages, dazzled by sunlight, the sidewalks were nearly deserted, and sometimes the lone sound came from moist blisters of chewing gum popping under my feet. The asphalt felt gummy, too, and its surface was speckled with bottle caps, coins and pencils that couldn't be pried up. Once I spotted a rubber shower clog stuck in the street like a brontosaurus footprint left centuries ago at the La Brea tar pits.

È cornuto! It astounded me to see the insulting gesture—index and little fingers extended like horns—everywhere. *Your wife has cuckolded you with a cabdriver.* In Italy that started family feuds, riots and gunfights, but here the horns were stenciled on store windows and restaurant menus, stitched on sweat shirts and plastered on the bumpers of cars and buses. Acting as my guide, Larry Sparks explained that this was the school symbol, *Hook 'Em, Horns* its rallying cry. The University of Texas team, the Longhorns, thundered into battle behind an enormous steer named Bevo. Burnt orange likenesses of Bevo, outfitted with fierce horns, were as ubiquitous as the *cornuto* sign.

Imbecile! The heat and horns I could handle. Yet what was I to make of the armadillos on billboards and on the walls of buildings, or embroidered onto shirts and pants? To me, the animal resembled a rat that had killed a turtle and commandeered its shell, but Larry said Texans felt a powerful affinity for it.

While I didn't share the emotion, I tried to accept it. I knew enough about myself and the unreliability of the human eye to concede that the Austin I saw might not be the bustling, vigorous city which two hundred and fifty thousand invincibly cheerful Texans believed they inhabited, might bear no relation at all to the wonders witnessed by the portly old ladies and gents who guided their portly new Pontiacs up and down the streets with the serenity of doges in their gondolas on the Grand Canal.

It was a relief when on my Duty Day I had to stay at the rectory answering the telephone, with no opportunity to probe and analyze my impressions of the past week. I was too busy repeating the hours for Masses and confession, explaining changes in the fasting rules and arranging baptisms, club meetings and Cana conferences for engaged couples.

My first difficult call came from a fellow having problems with a crossword puzzle. He needed a five-letter word which fit the clue "a religious case." I couldn't recall any recent legal issues involving the Church, but I asked around the rectory until someone still unknown and nameless to me hollered from the TV room, "Burse!"

"What case is that?"

"The case you carry the corporal in."

"Of course. Thank you, Father."

Then, late that afternoon as I was coasting toward dinner,

a woman called and sounded terribly upset. Anyone else might not have detected the telltale high notes of hysteria, but like a dog's my ears were attuned to a different frequency. When she said, "I need to speak to a priest," my stomach tightened, for I knew she truly did.

"I'm Father Amico."

"Marcia Hoover here. My husband and I don't live in your parish, Father. We're out near Mt. Bonnell. But our boy went to the University a while back and he attended St. Austin's every Sunday. At least, he promised he did. Anyway, Tommy, he doesn't live with us any more. He left home and became a . . . what they call a Jesus Freak. Now he lives in a commune off City Park Road and we're just worried sick about him. I mean, the way he talks and acts and dresses and doesn't communicate, he's like a zombie or something. So we've decided to have him deprogrammed, and we'd like a priest to be there."

"I'm new in town, and to tell you the truth I'm not sure St. Austin's does this sort of thing. Maybe you should send him to the Newman Club meeting next week, and I'll talk to—"

"You don't understand, Father. We can't send Tommy anywhere. If he knew what we were up to, he'd run off. And, you see, we're not asking you to do the deprogramming. We've hired a professional for that."

"I'm afraid this isn't my field, Mrs. Hoover. I'll have to speak with the pastor, and he's not here now."

"Well, when he comes back, tell him we'll be glad to pay your expenses and make an offering. You might mention we've got Noland Meadlow to do the job. Do you know him?"

"I'm new here," I repeated.

"Mr. Meadlow's national, not local. You must have read about him."

"I've been out of the country."

"He'll be at our house tomorrow afternoon. I'd like for you

to meet him. They tell me he's an awful interesting man and super bright."

"I'm sure he is. But I can't promise I'd be the one the pastor would send. I'll call you back after I talk to Father Ryan."

"I'd appreciate that. Because believe me, Father, desperate as we are to have Tommy home without all these sick ideas in his head, I don't want it to be without a Catholic influence."

"I understand," I said, although I hadn't any idea what she meant.

But that evening at dinner when I told Fr. Ryan and the others, they appeared to know at once what the woman wanted.

"Have you had any experience with Jesus Freaks?" Fr. Ryan asked me.

"No, but I've read about them. Aren't they part of this back-to-God movement among students?"

"Well . . . that's one way of putting it. As I recall, they weren't around much before you went to Rome. Politics was big back then. Now the fad is for the counter-culture to get into religion. You see them everywhere on the streets, singing and dancing, asking people if they've been saved and handing out pamphlets warning about the end of the world."

"Is that all? From the way Mrs. Hoover talked, it sounded a lot worse."

"Well . . ." Dragging out the word again, Fr. Ryan leaned back and looked at me as if what he had said should have been bad enough. "They must scare the bejabbers out of their parents. The kids have one-track minds, and everything they say or do is tied to Jesus. That may not sound bad, but what makes them a problem is they're out of contact with reality. The Church's position on these so-called Neo-Pentecostal groups is that they tend to be simplistic, overemotional, antirational, and because of the control their leaders have over the younger members, they can be dangerous."

Larry Sparks quietly interrupted. "Yes, I read that same

article in the Sunday *Messenger.* I don't mean to seem simplistic or antirational myself, but maybe it's a mistake to interfere. We don't agree on doctrinal or philosophical grounds with the Jesus Movement, but—"

"Philosophical grounds! Come on, Larry," Fr. Ryan said, "you know this isn't a theological question. These kids and their parents need protection. Unprincipled people are taking advantage. A lot of them, the rich ones, have been sweet-talked into donating money to the groups."

"Seems Biblical," Larry said. "Give all you own to the poor and follow Me. Like our parishioners letting us have their Green Stamps."

"I think if you'll reflect, you'll find what the Jesus Freaks are doing is a bit different from what the Bible recommends." Fr. Doyle smiled feistily, focusing on the brass medallion dangling from Larry's neck.

"Could be. That's hard to judge. I agree there are enormous differences between them and us." Larry spoke softly, careful to keep calm, and I was grateful not to be the one talking under Fr. Ryan's disapproving glare and Fr. Doyle's glinting teeth. "But do we want to set a policy of harassing people we don't approve of? The Catholic Church has come further than that, hasn't it? Look, I've been in contact with some of these kids. They may be misguided, but they do believe in God. Most of them lead good, clean lives, they stay off dope and they find tremendous strength in their faith. There's so much else for us to do, why bother them?"

"Generally, I wouldn't interfere with anybody's faith," Fr. Doyle said. "Not unless that faith makes it impossible for a person to function in the real world."

"Can Carmelites function in the real world? Who knows? My point is, Carmelites and other contemplatives have chosen not to, and we don't criticize them because we recognize they have a special calling. Maybe these kids have decided they can preserve their faith only by isolating themselves."

"That's a pretty elaborate defense of damn fools who run around with tambourines and zithers."

"While we run around in cassocks and Roman collars."

"Please, please." Fr. Ryan silenced Larry and Fr. Doyle. "We're getting off the subject. This woman didn't ask us to deprogram her son. She's hired somebody for that. But she'd like a priest to provide a Catholic influence. Am I right, Tony?"

"That's what she said."

"Who did they hire?" Larry asked.

"A man named Noland Meadlow."

"They must be serious, then," David Pernoski said. "I've read about him."

"What do they mean by 'deprogram'?" I asked.

"From what I've heard, Meadlow talks to these young people," Fr. Ryan said. "He reasons with them, reads passages from the Bible and points out how the Jesus Freaks have misinterpreted them."

"What gives him the right?" Larry demanded. "He's not a priest or minister."

"I didn't say I approve or disapprove. I don't know the man. What we have to do first, since these people seem set on bringing their son home, is get the facts straight. Then we'll see where we stand. Do we all agree on that?"

Fr. Doyle said yes. I heard David Pernoski's "Fer shir." The others nodded, while Larry, out of conviction, and I, out of confusion, remained silent and still.

"Okay, then. I suppose it's up to you to take care of this, Tony."

"Take care of it how?"

"I'd be glad to go in his place," Larry said.

"No, Tony answered the call. And he's the man we can spare at the moment." Fr. Ryan was weary of the argument. His scalp muscles sagged, smoothing the furrows from his forehead. "Go out there tomorrow and get a good reading on this guy Meadlow and find out what the parents have planned. As soon as you report back, we'll discuss it again. Now, if nobody minds, I'd like to hear Father Carver's report about this year's Newman Club program."

III

Next day I called a cab and waited at the curb in front of the church, roasting in my black suit. To settle my stomach and soothe my prickly skin, I was tempted to cross the street to the Night Hawk Restaurant—FAMOUS FOR TOP CHOP'T STEAKS. A TEXAS TRADITION SINCE 1932—but I feared someone from St. Austin's might spot me there, steeped in a sense of history and in the scent of fried food. So I stayed at my post, watching a sign on the University Bank which flashed the time and temperature. It was ninety-nine degrees. When the taxi showed up, I was soaked to the skin with sweat and started sniffling and sneezing in the air conditioning.

"Got a summer cold?" the cabby asked. "Murder, ain't they? Here, have a Kleenex." He waved one toward me. A lean, loose-jointed fellow, he then ground the car through its gears, giving dramatic flourishes with his elbow, an intricate ballet of his arm alone, all in time to the twang of the radio on which a country-western singer wailed the story of a guy who had caught his gal in the arms of another and shot them dead. Now trudging to the gas chamber, he was trying to cop a plea with the Lord.

We detoured from The Drag onto San Antonio Street and

drove past the Hillel House, where a sign had gone up for the oncoming semester: SHALOM Y'ALL AND WELCOME BACK TO U.T. GET YOUR FREE TICKETS FOR THE HIGH HOLY DAYS." The menorah under the message seemed to have lost its five middle branches. But no, that was the ubiquitous Longhorns symbol.

At Twenty-fourth Street we headed west, away from the clutter of the University, and coasted down past nine abandoned tennis courts where the green asphalt sent up wavering rays of heat. Though a parched wind shook the highest tree limbs, I couldn't hear it over the engine and the air conditioner. Then I sneezed explosively.

"Hey, you got it bad, don't you?" the driver said. "Sorry about the air conditioner. It's only got two speeds—off and on. That's better than the heater. It's got one speed—broken. Some days I freeze my butt off."

We crossed Lamar Boulevard and, soon afterward, Shoal Creek, no more than a trickle in its bleached gravel bed. Then we climbed uphill to an area of enormous tree-shaded homes where the lawns were broad, lush and close-cropped. This had to be one of the "nice neighborhoods" I'd been told about. Although I noticed no children playing in the streets or yards, I could imagine it as a marvelous place to be raised—here in the glittering suburbs that surrounded the emptiness at the center of the city like the honey-dipped crust of a doughnut.

"It's a miracle I ain't dead myself," the driver said as a new song, "Downwind of Your Love," twanged to life. "My head's stopped up half the time. And I about ruined my teeth what with eating crummy food, not brushing after every meal, and gulping gallons of sweet water."

"Sweet water?"

"Soda pop. All sorts. Coke, Pepsi, Dr Pepper. It settles your stomach and keeps you awake. 'Course, it eats the enamel off your teeth, but that's better than popping pills. One night I dropped a few reds and seen this gorilla grab the cab and shake it apart. Next thing I knew, the cops had me pinned to the ground and said I was under arrest for exceeding the speed limit across somebody's lawn."

The land began to buckle and roll—gradually at first in shallow valleys and low knolls, then in jagged rock ledges and promontories of pale limestone. The vegetation changed, too, turning scrubby and tenacious as it clung to the stone. While we labored uphill, the taxi coughed and sputtered and the air conditioning diminished. Cool air rushed over us again when we glided downhill, and I felt like I was having hot and cold flashes.

At my next sneeze, the driver said as if in reply, "Then there's customers climb into that back seat on dope or airplane glue or plain skunk drunk, and if I didn't protect myself I'd be out of business."

"I'll pray for your safety."

"Thanks, Reverend, but I can hold my own. Nobody messes with me without getting a good taste of the hose."

He seemed to expect a response. "I suppose that would humiliate them. You spray them, huh?"

"Nope. I hit them with this." From under his seat he pulled a two-foot section of garden hose, plugged by tape at either end. "It's filled with sand. Here, feel how heavy."

"I'll take your word for it. You ought to be careful. You wouldn't want to hurt anyone."

"Oh, a hose won't kill a man, but it'll sure keep him from climbing on you."

We had pulled onto Balcones Drive, another verdant glade of irrigated lawns and large split-levels sprawling over the broken landscape. Palms, cactus and agave plants partially screened the swimming pools and patios, and where the street came to a crest one piece of property was fenced off from the others by a stand of bamboo. The cabby found an opening in the foliage and we followed it through the green wickerwork jungle and up a circular drive canopied by live oaks.

In the distance stood a pink-brick Neo-Colonial house that had the raw look of something which had been built that morning and would be dismantled tomorrow. Since the trees had been cut back from it and the columns were nearly flush with the façade, there was no shade in the portico and the cluster of wrought-iron furniture was probably hot enough to leave a brand on your behind.

The front door opened when the taxi stopped, and a Doberman pinscher bounded out, pursued by a woman in white slacks and a sleeveless blue jersey. Catching the dog by the collar, she called to me, "Ask for a receipt."

The driver scribbled on a scrap of paper. "That's the best I can do for you."

"Thanks. Take care of yourself." I paid and tipped him from my pocket money, and gave the scrap of paper to the woman. "I'm Father Amico."

"Hi. Marcia Hoover."

The dog greeted me by sniffing up the inseam of my trousers until his growling snout was wedged in my crotch.

"Don't bother about him," she said. "He won't bite."

"But he breathes hard, doesn't he?" I tried to smile. "What's his name?"

"Ned. Why don't we go in before we melt?"

Without calling off the dog, she motioned for me to go first. I gently brushed past Ned, only to have him nuzzle me from behind as we entered a glacial hall. In the processed air I began sniffling again.

"Father, I can't tell you how grateful I am you agreed to come. Please sit down."

Ned and I made for the same chair. I reached it first, sat down and quickly crossed my legs. He laid his heavy head on my knee, drooling on my pants and glaring up at me with baleful black eyes.

"Like a drink, Father?"

"Just water. Or a glass of juice, please."

While the woman went into another room, I glanced away from Ned through a panel of tinted windows which took up an entire wall and gave a dramatic view of a cactus garden and a limestone hill that sloped down to a long body of water. On the far side of the lake there were higher hills dotted with A-frame houses, geodesic domes and cantilevered cottages perched on narrow terraces.

The room was furnished in what I assumed was Spanish Provincial. The dark-stained mahogany looked elegant and expensive, although after my quarters at the rectory a bus station would have looked luxurious. The upholstery had the smell of genuine leather, but that could have been Ned. I had lived in Italy long enough, however, to know the floor was authentic red tile. Mrs. Hoover's sandals clacked loudly as she returned with two glasses of grapefruit juice.

"Sure you wouldn't like something stronger?" she asked.

"No, it's too hot."

"I'll turn up the air conditioner."

"No, please don't," I said. The dog's head slipped from my knee and he barked.

"Ned, hush. Father, you said you're new to Austin. How do you like it?"

"It's very interesting. Are these the hills I've heard so much about?"

"I suppose so. They're the only ones between here and west Texas, about six hundred miles that way."

"They tell me people travel from all over to see them."

"Maybe they do. I never noticed."

At first glance she had looked younger than I'd expected, far too young to have a son in college. But on closer inspection, she showed her age in odd places—the roughness around her knuckles, the calluses on her feet, the wrinkles at the corners of her eyes and mouth. Though still a handsome woman, it appeared she had seen hard service in the past and her present difficulties were bringing back bad memories.

Ned raised his snout, growling.

"I bet that's Mr. Meadlow," she said, and headed for the door, followed closely by the dog.

She brought back a man who was so short the Doberman had to duck his head to find the fellow's crotch. The man was having none of that nonsense, however. With the flat of his hand he dealt Ned a hard crack across the muzzle. I feared the dog might attack, but he tucked tail and slunk over to where I stood.

"Mr. Meadlow, this is Father Amico."

"Glad to meet you," I said.

Meadlow didn't answer. Though he was as pale as something that had sprouted in a root cellar, he had a dry, firm grip and treated me to a blunt stare of appraisal. His grey eyes hesitated an instant at my belly, and he seemed to smile. Then he focused on my chest, as if meeting my gaze there. Considering his height, it was an understandable sort of stubbornness, this refusal to tilt his head and look up to anyone, but it unsettled me to have him speak directly at my sternum.

"What order are you?"

"Paulist."

"I've heard of the group. C.S.P. Does that mean Congregation of St. Paul or Can't Stop Preaching?"

Although it was an old joke, I obliged him with a smile. "Some say it stands for Congregation of Secret Protestants."

Meadlow reminded me of older priests I'd met. He wore the same shiny black Navy-surplus shoes, drab baggy trousers and a white short-sleeved, drip-dry shirt. Because he was so small and sinewy, and had hair that might have been silver or blond, it was difficult to estimate his age. Over fifty, I figured, but less than sixty.

"You ever done this before?" he asked.

"Done what?"

"A deprogramming."

"No."

"I didn't think so. You're out of shape."

"I'm waiting for the season to start."

As Meadlow glanced up at me from under inflamed eyelids, I decided I preferred to have him concentrate on my chest.

"Mr. Hoover's in his study. I know he's real anxious to meet you both."

With Mrs. Hoover in the lead, we left the room and came to a double door that appeared to be solid oak. Yet when she knocked, it sounded hollow as a solander and swung open before us. We went in, leaving the dog behind us in the hall.

Dressed in maroon double-knit slacks, white shoes, a wide white belt and a white and maroon checked polo shirt, Mr. Hoover had the golf pro look down to a tee, you might say. But he held an aluminum tennis racket and was flailing at a ball which was attached by an elastic cord to a red block of iron on the floor. The ball shot off the catgut at odd angles, zooming toward a panel of glass like the one in the living room, then bouncing back off the green carpet to Mr. Hoover's forehand or backhand. Only when Mrs. Hoover said, "Daddy, we're waiting," did he stop volleying.

"Really gives you a workout." Tossing the racket onto his desk, he yanked a handkerchief from his back pocket and mopped his scalp. Mr. Hoover was bald. He didn't have a receding hairline like Fr. Ryan. He had a gleaming, completely hairless head burnished by long afternoons in the sun.

He peeled a white mesh glove off his racket hand and shook with Meadlow. "Glad to meet you. I heard a lot about you. That was a real interesting interview on TV the other night. Hope you're still having luck with your work."

The little man nodded. "I wouldn't say it was luck, but we're making progress."

"Father Amigo, glad to meet you, too." He sandwiched my

fingers in his moist hands. "I reckon you could pretty well guess I'm not a Catholic. Me, I'm a . . . I used to be a Methodist, and you might could call me one now. But I'm not much of a churchgoer. I hold to my own private beliefs and they work fine for me."

"I see," I said.

He circled behind the desk, sat down and sipped from a highball glass. "Any of you all want a drink?"

"Got one." I rattled the ice cubes in my grapefruit juice.

"There's no liquor in that. I can tell from here that's Mama's bug juice."

"It's fine for me."

"Meadlow?"

The tiny man was peering through the panel of tinted windows at the cactus garden. "Soda. I'd like straight club soda."

Mrs. Hoover went to one of the walls of books, pressed a button and stepped aside as a whirring engine rotated the shelves. A well-stocked bar appeared. She handed the soda to me to pass to Meadlow and was about to press the button again when her husband said, "Might as well leave it open, Mama. Come on, sit down. Why don't you all pull a few chairs up to the desk? Looks like I got a couple of teetotalers on my payroll. But that's okay if it means we'll get this over with quick. Like I was saying, Father Amigo—"

"It's *Amico.*"

"Sorry, I never studied Spanish. Got a lot of Mexicans working for me, but I don't speak a word."

"The name's Italian."

"You don't say? I never studied that, either. Well, anyway, what I'm saying is I'm not a Catholic, but when Mama and me married, I signed the papers, and I'm a man keeps his promises. I sent my boy Tommy to church schools right on up through the twelfth grade. And a hell of a lot of good it did him or us."

"Daddy, don't talk that way."

"How do you expect me to talk after what we been through?"

"You don't have to be angry and insult Father Amico."

"I'm not insulting anyone. But you swore it was a stage he was going through. You said he was running off into one damn fool thing after another to see would we come trotting after him. Well, we let him do that, and look what happened."

"What *did* happen?" I asked, both out of curiosity and to calm Mr. Hoover.

"Father, I told you yesterday on the telephone," his wife said.

"You told me you were upset about the boy, but you didn't explain why. What's he done?"

Hoover took a long swallow, then stamped wet rings on the desk blotter with his glass. "I'll put it to you pure and simple, Reverend. We sent the boy to college up North and he hasn't been the same ever since. He got into everything going. I'm talking about civil rights, anti-war, acid rock, radical politics, marijuana, ecology. You name it, Tommy did it, and it like to drove us nuts. Then he got another wild hair, dropped out and transferred to U.T., talking about this Jesus business. After all those years of spouting catechism and saying rosaries and going to Mass, he claimed he'd been converted. Said he had the Lord in his heart and realized what he had to do."

"And what was that?"

Mr. Hoover snorted. "You tell me! All I see him doing is wandering around the city throwing away my money, warning folks about Satan and begging them to save their goddamn souls."

"Daddy, I asked you not to speak like that to Father Amico."

"Why not? He's a man, isn't he? Hell, he hears a lot worse in the confession box. Don't you, Father Amigo?"

"It's all right, Mrs. Hoover."

" 'Course it's okay. Religion's a good thing, but you gotta live in the real world. Now, that boy of mine . . ."

While Hoover described the real world he wanted everybody to live in, his scalp turned dark purple, registering the depths of his rage. I glanced at Noland Meadlow. Sitting with his knees clamped together and his palms jammed against them, he was doing isometric contractions. As the muscles in his arms and neck flexed, a net of veins, filling with blood, spread over them. He swiveled his head from side to side, and Hoover might have assumed Meadlow was responding to a question, but he was exercising his face, too. Like someone beset by terrible twitches, he squeezed his eyes shut, then shot them wide. He dropped his jaw and raised it, stretching the skin taut. Once, when he thought no one was looking, he leaned back, widened his mouth to its limit and let out a "silent scream." I had read that movie stars followed this regimen to maintain their muscle tone. But although he might have been strong, Meadlow didn't look particularly healthy. Occasionally, he dipped a finger into his glass to wet his red eyelids.

". . . what these damn kids need is a good war or depression to teach them the facts of life."

"You don't mean that, Daddy. You're upset." Mrs. Hoover turned to me, holding a hand to her chest. "You've got to understand what we've been going through, Father. Tommy's our only child and he was such a good, happy, cheerful boy. All his teachers said so. Even after those growing pains he went through at Yale, he was never a serious problem. Everything was fine until he joined the Jesus Freaks. They're the ones who changed him. Now he won't have anything to do with outsiders, not even us. Thaddeus turns them against their own families."

"Thaddeus?"

"The leader of Christ's Love Commune."

"The little shit who's stealing my money right out of Tommy's pockets," muttered Mr. Hoover through the teeth that bit at his thumb.

"It's not the money so much," Mrs. Hoover assured me. "It's how Tommy acts. He won't listen to anybody except Thaddeus, and he isn't interested in anything but religion. If you ask him to explain, he starts chanting or talking about Jesus or telling us how we should save our souls. He swears he won't come home until we repent and accept Jesus into our hearts.

"For God's sake, Father, I'm a Catholic and I try to be a good one, but that isn't enough for Tommy. I don't think he'll be happy unless we give away our home and go to live in the hills with him." Her eyes began to brim with tears. "You've got to help us, Father Amico. They've turned my boy into a zombie."

"I see, I see," I said to soothe her. "I'll do what I can."

"No, you don't see. You won't understand until you've been around him. It's like . . . like he's possessed."

"But by God, Mrs. Hoover, not the devil."

"God or devil, who gives a damn?" Meadlow said. "The point is, you people asked me to deprogram the boy and that's what I intend to do just as soon as I get the go-ahead."

"Now we're talking," Mr. Hoover said, heaving himself to his feet and striding unsteadily from behind the desk. "I admire a man doesn't waste my time. How you figure to do this?"

"I'm working on a game plan," Meadlow said. "I've had your son under surveillance now for a few days, and I've noticed a routine. Every afternoon he leaves the commune, walks along Lake Austin and heads up through the hills to a place off City Park Road where he *meditates.*" Meadlow spat the word out. Micturate, masturbate, meditate, they might all have been the same to him. "When he's strolling along up there—'blissed out,' as they say—I'll swoop down and nab him. I'll take him to a motel I know and talk sense to him for a while, then bring him home with his head screwed on right."

"You sound pretty sure of yourself." Hoover had picked up his racket and was practicing strokes without the ball.

"I *am* sure of myself and my technique. I've done over eighty deprogrammings and always got my man."

"I'm warning you, it won't be easy this time. From what I've seen of Tommy lately, it may take a brain transplant to set him straight."

"Daddy, that's a terrible thing to say."

"It's the truth."

"Look," I said, shifting uncomfortably in the chair, careful to hold my head away from Hoover's tennis racket, "isn't this illegal? I mean it sounds a lot like kidnapping."

"Don't you worry about that," Meadlow said. "They've tried to pin raps on a couple of deprogrammers, but couldn't make them stick."

"What about the Constitution and, you know, freedom of religion?"

"Whose side are you on, Amigo?"

"Really, Father," Mrs. Hoover murmured in a hurt voice, "weren't you listening when I described how he acts? That's not religion. That's craziness."

"Well, it's not your religion or my religion, but . . ."

"And on top of everything, he's living outside the sacraments in a state of mortal sin. Don't you want him back in the Church?"

"Of course, Mrs. Hoover, it would be fine with me if he returned to the Church. But you can't make a person stop believing one thing and start believing another."

"Want to bet?" Meadlow asked.

"I mean it's wrong to force him. You mentioned he was in college. How old is he?"

"Going on twenty-two."

"Don't you see, he's an adult. If you kidnap him and drag him away from the commune, brainwash his beliefs and bring him back home, you'll just be changing him from one kind of zombie to another."

"Who said anything about brainwashing?" Meadlow demanded.

"Call it what you like, it violates the boy's free will."

"What free will? Who has free will? Not this kid. Not after what he's been through," Meadlow said. "I know these groups, and that boy's brain is like jello by now. Jesus Freaks control their members by subliminal suggestion, hypnotism, Korean War–style communist brainwashing and a few old-fashioned Hitler Youth Movement techniques."

"My God, how are we ever going to save Tommy?" Mrs. Hoover asked.

Meadlow had won an advantage and took his time answering. "There's no fail-safe procedure, but our chances are good if we act quickly. Like I told you, I'll talk to the boy, reason with him. I know a little something about human nature and religion, and I believe I can convince him he's jumped the track. In my business you learn how to handle these kids or you don't last."

"For Chrissake, let the man do his job," Hoover said. "I'd just like to be sure about one point. Are you positive on our legal position? The last thing I need is some nosy lawyer flying down from New York and throwing my ass in jail for rescuing my own son. That Constitution business the Reverend mentioned seemed to ring a bell. If I remember right—"

"You'll remember the Constitution says Congress shall make no law concerning an establishment of religion, and it guarantees against interference by the federal government in an individual's freedom of worship—within certain limits. But—now, this is the important part—it doesn't say anything about personal or family interference. That's a grey area, and I've had good luck using it as a defense."

"I don't want to have to use any defense. Like I said, the

last thing I need is court costs on top of the money my son has forked over to every idiot in the state who owns a Bible."

"Look, I enjoy very good relations with law-enforcement agencies, especially here in Texas," Meadlow said. "Most of them put their men at my disposal, because they recognize there's ample justification for stepping in against these Jesus groups. You see, according to the experts, it's perfectly legitimate for the police to break the law in order to avoid a greater injury. Think how many times you've read about them moving in against churches and sects when there's reason to suspect they might harm an individual or society. They've indicted ones that practice polygamy, or oppose inoculation and medical care, or advocate rituals involving sexual aberrations and snake handling."

"Wait a minute," I broke in. "Nobody mentioned the boy's being involved in sexual aberrations or snake handling."

Meadlow shrugged. "Who knows what they're doing at that commune?"

Hoover whacked his leg with the racket. "That's for damn sure."

"I know," Mrs. Hoover said. "I've visited Tommy a couple of times."

"You never told me." Her husband sounded betrayed.

"I didn't want to upset you. But, Mr. Meadlow, it's just a big old house in the hills. Much as I wish Tommy didn't live there, they do seem to keep it clean. I didn't see any snakes or sex or that sort of thing."

"I didn't say you had. We're getting off the subject." He glowered at me. "Snakes and sex aside, what we have here is a family torn apart by extreme and irrational religious beliefs. If our system doesn't protect its citizens against that, what does it protect?"

"You don't have to convince me," Hoover said. "I thought all along we had a right to step in. How about you, Mama? I'd like Meadlow to get started before the boy goes too far off the deep end."

Mrs. Hoover had her hand at her bosom again. "What do you think, Father Amico?"

"Hard to say." Once more I shifted uneasily in the chair.

"Please, you have to help. I wouldn't feel right if a priest wasn't there with Tommy," she said, sounding as dubious now about Meadlow and the deprogramming as I was.

"Where do you intend to do this?" I asked the little man.

"South of here about two hundred miles."

"Would we be gone overnight?"

"Definitely."

"How long might we be away?"

"Depends on the boy. But I've never had one hold out longer than thirty-six hours."

"I'll have to ask the pastor's permission. That's out of our parish, probably out of the diocese. He might not let me stay away from the rectory."

"Why can't you talk to Tommy here at our house or somewhere in Austin?" Mrs. Hoover asked.

"That's not how I operate. It's not part of the program. I get better results moving these kids to a new environment where they can't depend on the emotional crutches that've been propping them up. Why do we need the priest, anyway?"

"Because," Mrs. Hoover said, "I believe in God."

The room went weirdly quiet. Mr. Hoover halted in mid-backswing. Meadlow glanced down and patted his flat stomach.

"Did you hear me, Mr. Meadlow? I believe in God and I'd like to have my son back without all his sick ideas, but still believing and not harmed in any way. I think Father Amico will be a big help."

"That's your business. I'll free him from the Jesus Freaks and interface with him for a few days to make sure he doesn't run right back to them. After that, it's up to you how he's handled."

"When do we start?" Hoover asked, following through on his stroke, visibly relieved that we were no longer discussing God.

"Soon as the priest's ready."

"I'll ask the pastor this afternoon." Rapidly I was reappraising my feelings in the light of Mrs. Hoover's fervent declaration of faith.

"One other thing. What about this money my boy's been doling out?" Hoover picked up the tennis ball, swatted it and sent it streaking toward the tinted window. The elastic cord lashed it back for a low volley. "How do I go about getting it?"

"You say it's your money?" Meadlow asked.

"You better believe it."

"Well, in a manner of speaking," Mrs. Hoover said. "Most of it came from Tommy's grandmother, my mother."

"A trust fund?" Meadlow asked.

"No, he inherited it on his twenty-first birthday."

"And I gave him a big chunk of running-around money right after he quit Yale," Hoover said. "Far as I can tell, he sunk some of it into that house and a tractor and enough food to stake those creeps for a few months. But there must be a lot left. So how do we get it back?"

"You don't." Meadlow set aside his soda glass. "From what you've said, the money belongs to the boy. He's of age and can do whatever he wants with it."

"You mean you'll grab my son, but you won't go after my goddamn dough?"

"Money's a different matter. The law's a lot tougher about recovering cash. It's not my line of work, anyway. Hire a lawyer. Maybe you could have the kid declared mentally incompetent."

"Daddy, you wouldn't."

"Don't bet on it. We're talking here about a big wad of bread."

"No, what we're doing is spinning our wheels," Meadlow said. "In my opinion, you won't get that money. Even if you declared him incompetent, even if he seems insane to us, a judge might not agree. You'd better write it off."

"Son of a bitch!" As his scalp quilted and empurpled, Hoover swung the racket wildly and it slipped out of his hand, spinning like an airplane propellor toward the Thermopane window. Its impact spread a spider web over the glass. The racket hung there a second before dropping to the carpet, followed by tinkling fangs of glass.

Mrs. Hoover quickly recovered her composure, as if she were on easy terms with her husband's anger. "Will you please wait in the garden while I speak to Daddy?"

"Daddy" was slumped behind his desk as she showed us to a door leading to a sun deck and down a flight of stairs to the garden.

"Sickening display," Meadlow muttered.

"I can't believe it."

"Why not? You see stuff like that every day."

"I don't."

"You would in my job."

"The man must be mad."

"Depends on your definition. But one thing's certain. He's been programmed his whole life to assume he'll get what he wants if he acts irrationally. Now they're shocked that their son does the same thing. What do they expect when the whole family reinforces its members in irrational behavior?"

I followed as he strode away from the house along a gravel path between the outcroppings of cactus, and while I was already sweating, Meadlow looked dry and blanched as the caliche underfoot.

"But, you know," he continued in a lecturing, hectoring

voice, "much as they deny it, men like Hoover crave discipline. They're secretly crying out for someone to set limits, because irrationality pits a person against himself. It's like having one foot on solid ground and the other in quicksand. Sooner or later, it splits you smack up the middle."

"I suppose you consider religion a kind of quicksand."

"What else would you call it? It's illogical itself and leads to more of the same. Imagine the sort of society you create when one of the primary agencies for behavioral reinforcement—religion—encourages illogical thought and action. We try to counteract it with massive doses of last-ditch logic—the law, criminal courts, imprisonment, capital punishment—but by then it's too late. You need consistent reinforcements from the start."

I let loose a condescending chuckle like one of those I had heard jesuitical debaters use. "Could be a semantic conflict, Meadlow. Maybe what you call consistent and rational is what I'd call evil."

"It wouldn't surprise me, Padre, if you called your ass your elbow."

I was reaching—fumbling, really—for a retort when Meadlow spotted something and quickened his pace. Ahead of us, a young black man, the gardener, crossed the path carrying a pair of pliers and began tweezing out spines from the prickly pear cactus. The spiky tufts of his Afro were spackled with what looked like jewels.

Meadlow stood squinting at him, hands on hips, apparently hard-pressed to stay patient. "What's that on your hair?"

The gardener glanced over his shoulder as if somebody might be behind him. "You talking to me, man?"

"Who else? I asked what's on your hair."

"Ice. Pieces of ice."

"Ice!" Meadlow let his hands fall and slap his thighs.

"It's hot out here," he said, suddenly sheepish.

"Sure it's hot. And you're working hard." Meadlow spoke in a softer voice. "But what does the man up in that house think when he watches you diddy-bopping around with chunks of ice in your hair? He thinks here's some simple jive-ass I can pay peanuts to."

"I get good money."

"Don't bullshit me. I know better. I'm here to help. Don't you see, every time you wear that crap on your head it's as bad as breaking into a buck and wing. You gotta watch the way you come on. Pride, that's the image to project."

The gardener shook his head, shedding the ice.

"That's better. What's your name?"

"Ronald."

"Glad to meet you." Meadlow clasped his hand. "Do you have a driver's license, Ronald?"

The man nodded.

"You look like you're in good shape. Are you strong?"

"Strong enough."

"I may be able to use a man like you. Here's my card." He produced one from his wallet. "I'll call you next time I'm in Texas. Let's keep in touch."

"Sure, man."

"Now get back to work and do a good job."

As we retraced our steps toward the house, I asked, "Do you plan to hire the guy or something?"

"The odds are against it, but I like to help people and have them primed and in position—just in case. You take that fellow. A few words of encouragement can make all the difference. You just have to talk sense."

"What are you, anyway?" I asked.

"A deprogrammer."

"A hypnotist, you mean."

"I don't hypnotize people. I dehypnotize them."

"What's the difference?"

"Stick around. You'll see."

"Where do you live?"

"Wherever I am. I go where I'm called."

"Must be a busy life."

"It is. There aren't many of us around."

"No doubt about that. What's in this for you, Meadlow?"

"Satisfaction."

"And a lot of money, I imagine."

"Imagine whatever you want."

At the stairway to the sundeck we met Mrs. Hoover, who was blinking back tears. A lock of hair lay across her damp cheek like a charcoal smudge. "You'll have to forgive Daddy. He's been under an awful strain. You see how badly we need your help."

"I'm ready," Meadlow said. "It's up to the priest."

"I'll talk to the pastor and call you, Mrs. Hoover."

"Remind him we're willing to make an offering."

"I will."

Brushing back her hair, she asked Meadlow, "Have you and Daddy discussed the financial arrangements?"

"There's nothing to discuss. I have a set rate."

"What's that?"

Shooting me a sidelong glance, he said, "Tell you later."

"I have to know now."

"It's not what you think. I'm not trying to trick you."

"I'm sure you're not, but Daddy'll ask me and if I don't have the figures he'll get angry again."

"I work for expenses."

"That's all?"

"That's all." He avoided my eyes.

"There must be some mistake. We don't want you to work for nothing."

"There's no mistake. And don't worry about me. I can take care of myself." Meadlow stiffened. "I have to be going."

"So do I," I said. "Would you please call a cab?"

"Oh, I'm sure Mr. Meadlow will drop you off. He goes right by St. Austin's."

Meadlow studied his shiny black shoe tops.

"I don't like to put him to any trouble. He's a very, very busy man."

"It's no trouble. Is it, Mr. Meadlow?" She dipped forward to look him in the eye.

The deprogrammer drove a black stripped-down Chevy. "A priest's car," I chided him.

"It's rented," he said, revving the tinny engine.

"Of course, but from the chancery office."

As we pulled away, Ned tore loose from Mrs. Hoover on the porch and loped after the car, barking and snapping at the tires.

"You dress like a priest, too," I said. "Maybe you have a vocation and won't admit it."

Meadlow was watching the dog in the side-view mirror, and as we descended the driveway lined by live oaks, he drifted to the left, close to the thick-trunked trees, while Ned darted and retreated and darted again, outraged by his reflection in the hubcap. I was about to say something when Meadlow cut the distance closer, all but brushing the trees. Suddenly, with a sickening thud, the Doberman smashed head-on into a live oak and fell in his tracks. I turned to see Ned stagger upright, fumble in a circle, then sink down again.

"What are you, crazy? Why did you do that?"

"Do what?" he asked innocently.

"Was it because I kidded you about your clothes and your car? Don't tell me you didn't do it on purpose."

"Everything I do has a purpose, Padre. What I've never understood are people who lack a sense of purpose." He had fallen into his lecturing voice. "You take dogs and cats, all pets. For centuries man has struggled to separate himself from the animals. Now, like idiots, after kicking them out of our caves, we drag them right into our living rooms, lavishing food and attention and a perverted love on them. What's the purpose of that?"

"Great excuse, Meadlow. But it won't wash. I bet you're afraid of animals because you can't control them."

"For Chrissake, spare me the two-bit psychoanalysis. Maybe a Great Dane scared my mother before I was born. Maybe I saw her doing it doggy-style with my father. What does that shit add up to? Isn't it enough that dogs are smelly, dirty, and they bite?"

"And so you run them into trees?"

"You don't believe it, put the wires on me and I'll take a polygraph test." Wrenching the wheel, Meadlow gunned the Chevy down Balcones Drive.

"It doesn't matter what I believe, Meadlow. But if you're lying to yourself—"

"I'll go to hell, right? I'm not sweating that."

"Who knows where you're going? But while you're getting there you'll be operating under as many illusions as anybody else."

"That's your opinion."

"I do have a right to one, don't I?"

"Right? Everybody yammers about rights. What do they mean?"

"It means two can play this game. Why don't you accept money for what you do? Trying to impress me with your charity?"

"I don't believe in personal charity."

"But you must be some sort of an idealist. And that doesn't fit in with your obsession for logic and rationality."

"I don't believe in idealism, either."

"That doesn't mean it doesn't exist. Look, Meadlow, I think by doing these deprogrammings for free, you're acting just as irrational as the people you criticize."

"I told you I have my reasons."

"People in asylums say that."

"I don't intend to trade insults with you." On Thirty-fifth Street he swung left, the rear end swerving and squealing on the soft asphalt. "I've got plenty of money to last me the time I have left."

"Every man's time is short."

"Cut the Biblical crap, Padre. I keep my body ready, and I can depend on it. But I'm sixty-two years old and I've got a lot of work to finish. It's already hard to convince people to listen. I'm not about to blow any chances by demanding money. The poor deserve deprogramming as much as the rich. Maybe more. You don't charge for what you do. At least you're not supposed to. Why should I? I've always led my life in a certain way and I want to carry on exactly the same until the end. If I let side issues interfere, I'm liable to lose my focus. And believe me, when concentration is crucial, money and death are nothing but distractions."

"No, I'd say the threat of death ends the superficial distractions and forces you to reconsider."

"Reconsider what? Nothing! It's a mistake to think death matters." He sat up straighter, as if determined to inject strength into his sixty-two-year-old spine. "Why complicate things? Man is really a simple organism. Once you accept that and adjust yourself to the idea that we're here because we evolved haphazardly from elemental chemical compounds by a process of natural selection, it's remarkable how many problems are reduced to insignificance."

We sped down Windsor Road and crossed Shoal Creek, and although the land had flattened I felt I was still on a roller coaster. Having hurried for years to accidents, hospitals and sickbeds, I thought I knew as much as anybody about death and the desire to find a stratagem for accepting or ignoring it. But strangely this little man didn't invite expressions of empathy and he didn't allow himself any emotion.

"Where does the boy, this Jesus Freak, fit in?"

"Don't you see? It's all connected. My ideas, the deprogrammings."

"No, I don't get it. One minute you seem to have a lot of serious questions on your mind. The next minute, you're planning to kidnap some pathetic boy. No matter how much you disagree with his beliefs, he isn't hurting anyone."

"You're wrong, Padre. He hurts a lot of people, including himself. I have to save him and others before they do more damage. That way each of them'll become a potential deprogrammer, someone to carry on the work when I'm gone. I once read a book about a desert tribe in Africa that sends men out from the safe areas to explore the empty quarters and set up advance settlements. Each generation pushes on a little farther until by now they've damn near covered the whole desert. Pretty soon there won't be a blank spot on the map and nobody'll stumble around blindly, worshiping wind and water. That's how I look at my job."

"You and I may have read the same book. It's about the bushmen of the Kalahari. I based a sermon on it, begging for vocations. I said we need priests to spread the word of God through a desert-like pagan world."

"You get a flood of conversions?"

"Not that I noticed. What about you? Where's your flock?"

"I'm not looking for lambs. The world needs leaders."

"I couldn't agree more. But what are you and your disciples pushing?"

Meadlow gave me a quizzical glance. "No, Padre, you're not interested. You've got a closed mind."

"Try me. It'll tone up your muscles."

"Well, it's not easy to explain, but . . ." But of course he would do it anyway. As I was to discover time and again, it required very little to get him going, and whenever he discussed his vocation he carefully balanced phrases and clauses, paused at commas, stopped at periods and seldom stumbled or rambled. "When I was in the Marines, and then later with the Los Angeles Police Department, I did a lot of work with computer technology. Matter of fact, my last assignment was to make a proposal for computerizing military and police operations throughout the country.

"What shocked me was how much ignorance and resistance my report exposed. People kept accusing me of wanting to replace humans with 'mechanical brains,' of advocating a corps of robots. The newspapers were always howling about the threat of Orwellian horrors and *1984*. The usual hogwash. Computers just happen to have a higher rate of speed and accuracy than most humans. I was simply suggesting it might be smart for men to imitate some aspects of machines. What's wrong with that?"

"I didn't say anything. I'm listening."

"One thing you'll have to admit is that machines never act emotional. They never become dangerous or destructive because they're flustered. When they don't have the correct information, they shut down. Simple as that. You get out of them what you put into them. Follow me?"

"I still don't see where the Hoover boy fits in."

"I'm getting to that. After all this work with computers, I asked myself whether the same methodology couldn't carry over to the human mind. I thought maybe if you controlled the input you could control and predict the output. So I experimented on myself for a few months and the results were amazing. I learned you can eliminate daydreaming, nonproductive downtime, and even so-called emotional problems, because, you see, the human brain is a perfect servomechanism, a complete circuit system containing everything necessary to its survival and success."

"What happens when it blows a fuse?"

"What the hell kind of silly question is that?"

"I'm serious. You said the brain is perfect, complete, and contains everything necessary to its survival. How's that true if it doesn't last?"

"Look, I work on the assumption that input determines output. If we controlled what went into people, we could—"

"What? Control death?"

"Can't you forget death for a minute? We could make life a lot more productive if we applied computer technology to human behavior."

"Oh, come on, Meadlow."

"No, listen. I've programmed all the most important problems, and in each case I showed how things could be improved. You take marriage. As an institution it's a social, financial and psychological wipe-out. We've either got to get rid of it or find out why it fails so often."

"Do a print-out on infidelity, selfishness, illness, irritability, incompatibility . . ."

"You're missing the point. You're depending on subjective opinion when what we need is hard data. Like Masters and Johnson. They quantified human sexual behavior, and that was a step in the right direction. But what about money? According to the polls, that's the number one marital problem. We make people get licenses and blood tests. Why not require engaged couples to pass courses in economics? I have figures that prove a single seminar in bookkeeping would reduce the probability of divorce by seven percent."

"Thank God I became a priest. I never got beyond algebra. Here's the church."

Meadlow pulled over to the curb. "I'm not finished."

"I'm sure we'll discuss this again. I have to report to Father Ryan."

"Yeah, okay, talk to your boss. I'll call you tonight. I'd like to start tomorrow." Then, as I was sliding out, he caught my coattail. "One more thing . . ."

I turned to the pale little man who, now that he'd told me his age, had begun to look it.

"I don't want you going in there and praying for me."

"What are you talking about?"

"Make damn sure you don't do any pleading for the salvation of my nonexistent soul."

"If it's nonexistent, why worry?"

"You heard me, Padre."

"You'll never know, will you?"

To keep him guessing, I pulled loose and went into the church rather than the rectory. Yet, once inside, I lost my momentum and couldn't bring myself to approach the altar, kneel and pray. I lingered far back in the Crying Room, where on Sunday mornings mothers with colicky children sat through the Mass behind thick plates of glass and observed the Holy Sacrifice as if on an immense television screen.

Though I had never met one before, I'd heard of men like Meadlow—men madly involved with the idea of God. Eager as they were to stamp out religion, they at least took it seriously, and some theologians thought that atheists stood a short step from belief. Still, it occurred to me that while Meadlow might secretly wish to be saved, I wanted something from him as well. He was as anxious to argue eschatology as anyone I had met since the seminary, and even when he angered me I was drawn to him. Fighting the little man, I felt I was fighting myself, for the questions he raised were ones I had already asked. The answers he offered were those I had considered. Although I hadn't forgotten Mrs. Hoover's desire for a Catholic influence, I realized the main reason for wanting to go on the deprogramming was to reach a conclusion about myself. If what remained of my faith couldn't survive several days' exposure to Noland Meadlow, it was pointless, I thought, to delay the inevitable for six months.

* * *

Leaving the church by the side door, I spotted Fr. Ryan bustling out of the rectory with a bamboo fishing pole. Flies and lures festooned the band of his beat-up fedora.

"Hello there," he hailed me. "Fish are biting at Lake Travis."

He would have kept on going if I hadn't hollered that I needed permission to be away from the rectory and out of the parish overnight. Assuming, that is, St. Austin's wanted me to participate in the deprogramming.

"Hmmm." He stopped and held the bamboo pole like a crosier. "How did the situation strike you?"

"Very bad. The family's had a tough time and is determined to go through with this. The Hoovers would like me to be along."

"They did say they'd pick up the tab, didn't they?"

"Yes. And make an offering. I think they can afford it."

"How about this man Meadlow? He must be pretty sharp."

"He is. And hard. I'm sure he's capable of doing the job, but the parents are right to want a third party, a priest, there."

"Why's that?"

"The Catholic influence. Meadlow's an atheist. I don't believe the boy should be left to him alone."

"Hmmm," Fr. Ryan hummed again, and as the ladder of furrows climbed his lofty forehead, I feared I had overdone it and he would deny me permission or send someone in my place. But finally he said, "You'd better go along, then. Father Sepak will handle your hospital duty. The rush doesn't start until the students show up. We'll manage for now. And, ah, look . . ." He directed his eyes toward his feet, where he was tapping the pole on the concrete. "I don't think there's any need to consult the others. We won't mention it, all right?"

I was surprised he hadn't asked more questions and didn't care to discuss the subject at dinner, but perhaps this secrecy didn't amount to anything. Maybe he was simply weary of conflict. "All right," I said.

Fr. Ryan raised his head. "Be on the alert down there. I'd like a full report on Meadlow's technique. This type of case is bound to keep cropping up. Next time, we'll take care of it ourselves."

IV

The hills fell away from us in soft grey and green folds, and far below, at the bottom, the lake gleamed a darker green. A gusting breeze had built tall thunderheads to the south and brought through the open windows the smell of cedar, sage and mesquite. Though the hills couldn't have been higher than a few hundred feet, they humped up out of the flat land like the Himalayas. As we sat in the Chevy at the side of City Park Road waiting for Tommy Hoover, I felt for the first time since arriving in Texas that I was truly in the West, far off in the mountains.

"This is beautiful," I said, hoping the view would soothe my nerves.

Noland Meadlow was hunched behind the steering wheel doing isometric contractions, and the strain had pinched a bit of color into his normally pallid complexion. Grunting, he glanced around. "Scrubland. Full of scorpions, snakes and armadillos."

"Really? I'd like to see one."

"What, a rattler?"

"Anything wild."

"You came across a big fat diamondback, you'd change your

mind damn quick." But he let go of the wheel and took a second, slower look. "It is nice here. Wonder who owns it? The way Austin's growing, they're holding a hell of a piece of real estate."

"Is that all you think of when you see something this lovely? Property, subdivisions, money?"

"For Chrissake, not a sermon. If you're trying to convert me by praising God's grandeur, forget it. It's been done before."

"Are you a Catholic?" I asked, following a hunch I'd had since yesterday.

Meadlow's mouth curled into a faint smile. "Twice over."

"Meaning what?"

"Meaning I was baptized a Catholic two times."

"Are you a priest?" I pursued this wilder hunch, having found fallen-away priests some of the most rabid priest-baiters.

"Don't be ridiculous."

"Well, I still don't see why you were baptized twice. It doesn't make sense."

"You'd have to ask my mother. She's the one who didn't make sense. And she's dead now."

"I'm sorry."

Gazing out at the hills, the deprogrammer probed, then massaged his left biceps. "Actually, I was baptized a lot more than twice. When I was a kid, my mother hauled me all across the country converting to one religion after another. She didn't believe in that bullshit any more than I do, but that's how we lived. After we were converted and christened, we'd throw ourselves on the mercy of the congregation. What could they do? They'd just been jabbering at us about faith, hope and *charity.* How could they refuse when we begged for help? Let me tell you, the Mormons, not the Catholics, were the most generous ones we met. Or maybe the dumbest. We joined up with them nine times—in different cities, of course—and never got sent off empty-handed."

"Your mother must have been—"

"A bum," Meadlow said. "A bona-fide deadbeat."

"No, not that. Frantic to find a way to support you."

"Why didn't she work? No, she was a wild woman, a hippie before they had a word for it. It gave her more satisfaction to screw somebody out of a dime than to earn a dollar. And she was addicted to everything before it became chic. Drugs, sex, drinking, food, astrology—you name it. Never even tried to control herself. 'Anything worth doing is worth overdoing,' that's what she used to say." Meadlow had his hands on the wheel once more, pressing and pulling, priming his muscles. After the first flood of words, he seemed to have regained a firm grip on his feelings. "In the end, she was an old, fat, messy woman. About your size, come to think of it. She stayed in bed all day eating Red Hots and drinking J.T.S. Brown. Finally drowned in her vomit."

"That's awful. It sounds like she was, ah, you know, disturbed."

"No. Just a slob."

"You shouldn't talk like that about your mother. I'm sure you had some feeling for her."

"Yeah, revulsion."

"I don't believe that, Meadlow." As a matter of fact, I did believe it, but I was desperate to discover a single human impulse we shared. "You shouldn't judge her so harshly. You don't know what she went through, what pressures were working inside her."

"It doesn't matter what's inside people. There I agree with the Bible. 'By their works shall you know them.' And then you have to judge them. Otherwise, you'll wind up like them—a worthless wreck."

"It's fine to recognize where she went wrong. Maybe you won't make the same mistakes. But you don't have to hate her."

"I don't hate her," he said. "That's not an emotion I allow myself."

"What about your father?" I asked, groping for other pieces to the puzzle. "What's he like?"

"I wouldn't know. He got tired of the religious hustle and left. He has to be dead by now. He'd be in his eighties."

"Didn't it ever occur to you, considering how your mother lived and how your father left, that your attitude toward religion and this boy might be a manifestation of—"

"There you go again with the penny psychology." He slapped the steering wheel.

"No, I just thought your feelings—"

"I don't have feelings. Not the type you're talking about. I respond to what I can see and touch. The only abstractions I accept are facts, figures and statistics. I refuse to commit myself one inch ahead of the scientific evidence. You don't believe that, put the wires on me."

Though I knew it would prolong the argument at a time when I preferred to stay calm and prepare for what was ahead, I couldn't keep from reminding him that scientists often acted on theories before they had all the information or absolute proof.

"That's their business," he barked. Then he corrected himself. "That's different. What I'm against is the kind of mumbo-jumbo you people—and psychiatrists—depend on. Hocus-pocus and all that crap! Look at Latin. For centuries it kept people in your pocket. But as soon as you spoke plain English, the jig was up. They understood what you were saying, knew it was nonsense, and split."

"I don't think that's why they left the Church."

"Why, then? You do admit they're leaving in droves, don't you?"

"Sometimes we failed them. We were too busy with less important things. Other times they failed themselves—they abused their faith. Faith is a gift, you know, and once it's gone, it's hard to get back."

"Let me pass you a bulletin, Padre. You're not about to get those people back. They've wised up and realize they can count on reason and science."

"You think they understand that any better than they understood Latin? Science, that's the real mumbo-jumbo of domination today, not religion. When a scientist is speaking, people swallow whatever he says. How's that different from Church dogma?"

"Science is the truth. That's the difference. Whatever it claims, it can prove."

"We used to have proofs, too," I said, "and Catholics listened and believed them. But then something got switched around and you couldn't count on their believing Sunday followed Saturday."

"Look, science isn't based on what anybody believes, and it won't fold just because a few knuckleheads ignore it."

"I see. Then you're claiming it's like God, who's there whether we believe in Him or not. You can stamp out belief in this one poor boy, but God'll still exist."

"For Chrissake, let's cut this bullshit. We need to talk tactics. Tommy'll be up here in a minute, and I want you to slide over and take the wheel while I grab him. I can handle him once I catch him, but if he runs for it you'll have to follow us."

"I don't drive."

"You're kidding me." Meadlow angrily shoved his hair back. "You're doing this to screw me up."

"No, it's true. I never learned."

"What good are you, anyway?"

"In case you're not aware of it, I didn't come along as your chauffeur. I'm here to provide a Catholic influence."

"Whatever the hell that is! How am I supposed to drive and grab the boy at the same time?"

"Why don't you drive and I'll catch him?"

He threw back his head in a variation on the silent scream —the soundless guffaw. "You couldn't run from here to the corner without fainting. Even if you caught him, how could you hold him? You're lucky to hold your own water. Listen, there's nothing to driving. The car's got automatic. Just put it in gear and step on the gas."

"No!" I was fed up with his insults.

"Okay, climb in back. I'll drag him to the car and throw him in with you. I'm counting on you to keep him still. Sit on him if you have to."

I flung myself out of the front seat, slamming the door, then flopped into the back and slammed that door, too.

"Oh, shit," Meadlow said, "you're not going to sulk, are you? I have enough to do without worrying about your tender feelings."

"What do you expect after the way you talk? You treat people like dirt."

"I'm telling the truth. You *are* fat."

"And you *are* short," I blurted. "Absurdly short. You're almost a midget."

He went rigid and the nape of his neck burned brick-red.

"You can dish it out, but you can't take it."

"That's not fair," he said, swiveling around to face me. "I can't change how short I am. I make the best of the equipment I've got."

"Maybe I do, too."

"I doubt that. You Catholics call the body the temple of the Holy Ghost, but look at yours. It's more like the Astrodome than any temple. You could use a bra."

I lowered my eyes. My belly bulged beneath a floral sport shirt, my thighs had been shoved sausage-tight into beige summer-weight trousers. Even my hands and fingers were fat. "So what? It's comfortable."

"Comfortable! If I was your bishop, I'd want my men lean and mean, not comfortable. How can you do your duty when you're lugging around all that extra baggage? In the Marine Corps we'd have run your ass ragged. It's for your own good I'm saying this. The body and the brain, they're one muscle. You have to train it, punish it. You shouldn't give in."

"Give in to what?"

He paused a beat and blinked. "Don't give in to anything. I tell you what. To show I'm looking after your best interests, not just riding you, as soon as we're down south I'll start you on a simulated Marine Corps training program. I guarantee you'll lose weight and feel much better. It should sharpen up your mental processes, too. How about it?"

"I'll think it over," I said, still smoldering.

"Yeah, do that." He turned around to stare through the windshield. "One more thing. I'm not a midget."

"I didn't mean to hurt your feelings."

"You didn't hurt me. Nobody can. But you're mistaken about dwarfs and midgets. I'm five feet four, so I'm nowhere near being a midget. And my physique is perfectly formed, so I'm sure not a dwarf. I just happen to be small. Is that clear?"

"Clear," I said. "But I think you ought to admit what you said about me was—"

"Now, when this kid comes up here, be on your toes. The trick is for me to catch him before he has a chance to hurt himself or us."

"Hurt himself how?"

"Fighting, thrashing around."

"Why didn't you warn me about this? Do the Hoovers know the danger?"

"They're not dumb. I'm sure they didn't think I was going to coax him into the car with candy."

"Have you injured any of these people before?"

"A few bruises. That's all. But one of them busted my thumb and another chipped my tooth."

"My God, it's a wonder somebody hasn't been killed. You should have told me."

"Shut up! There he is," Meadlow hissed.

"What? Where?"

"Shhh. There."

A tall, lean fellow stepped away from the scrubby forest of cedars and onto the road. Tommy Hoover was dressed like a day laborer in muddy laced-up boots, khaki pants and a grey work shirt. But he had a bushy red beard as broad as a shovel, and that, along with thin sandy hair and a sprinkling of freckles, added a dash of color and character to his face.

Meadlow climbed out of the car. "Excuse me. We're having engine trouble. Could you lend us a hand?"

"Glad to." The boy smiled. He had a sweet, benign expression. His meditation must have gone well today. "What's the problem?" he asked.

"The battery, it sounds like."

Tommy took a few steps forward, and his expression changed abruptly when he got a closer look at Meadlow. "White Death!" he shouted, and bolted for the trees, then shied away from them and galloped down the deserted road, his long arms and legs flying in different directions.

Meadlow sprinted in a straight line, working for an angle, anticipating where the boy would wind up. He quickly closed the last few yards and collided with Tommy from the blind side. The boy was surprised to see him there so suddenly. Meadlow seemed surprised, too, but it was the impact that knocked them away from each other.

Lunging, the little man grabbed Tommy's belt, leaned back and tried to dig in his heels. The leather soles of his Navy-surplus shoes skidded over the asphalt. That slowed the boy down, and Meadlow slipped an arm around his waist and hoisted him off the ground so that Tommy's feet pedaled air.

Meadlow gave the boy a rough shake to straighten him out, then caught an elbow to the forehead as he pulled him toward the car. But it was Tommy who faltered, as if to offer an apology. Meadlow never slowed down, and, tiny as he was, he looked like an ant dragging a twig twice its size.

"Open the door!" he called.

I scrambled out and held the door wide.

"No, get in and get ready to grab him."

"Praise Jesus. Praise Jesus. Please God, help me," the boy babbled, roiling about.

At the Lord's name, I froze.

"Move." The deprogrammer bumped me with his hip. "Hurry. I'm losing my hold on him."

I crawled into the back seat, and Meadlow shoved the twisting, sweating, shouting boy onto my lap. But he used my belly to bounce away from me.

"Hang on to him!" Meadlow hollered.

"Calm down. It's okay," I said, throwing my arms around him. "I'm a priest. I'm here to help you."

He rolled onto the floor and squirmed halfway out of the car. His legs scissored and kicked, his fingers clawed at the gravel. When one of his flailing, booted feet walloped me in the thigh, I let out a loud yelp more from surprise than pain. The boy quit thrashing, and his prayers and imprecations stopped as he glanced up to see whether I was hurt. Meadlow forced him off the floor and onto the seat.

"This is kidnapping," Tommy protested in a voice ragged from anger and exertion. "You won't get away with it. They'll catch you."

"Who'll catch us? Your parents hired me, the cops agree with what we're doing. There's no sense screaming and carrying on." Meadlow slammed the door.

"Don't worry," I assured him. "We just want to talk to you."

"That's right," Meadlow said, scooting behind the steering wheel and starting the car. "We're going to have a nice long talk."

"Where are you taking me?"

"On a little trip. Sit tight and admire the scenery."

"But where? Wait a minute. What about my friends at the house? I have to tell Thaddeus." He grabbed at Meadlow's shoulder as the Chevy swung onto the road.

"Get him off my back before he runs us over a cliff."

I hauled the boy down beside me. "Please, relax. Everything's all right. I told you, I'm a priest."

"Why are you taking me away from my friends?"

"You know why," Meadlow said. "Your parents tried to talk sense to you, and you wouldn't listen. Now it's my turn."

"It's none of their business what I do. It's not yours, either."

"I'll decide that."

"And you, you're letting him do this." He whirled on me, his green eyes wide. He had inherited something of his father's temper, as well as a scalp that registered outrage in purple hues. "Don't you know who he is? Noland Meadlow, White Death. He destroys souls."

"Nothing will happen to you while I'm here," I said.

"You don't believe me. You don't care whether he steals my soul."

He lunged for the door, shoved it open and tried to roll out onto the macadam. But I had him by the belt, and although I couldn't reel him in I held tight and shouted until Meadlow brought the car to a stop and hurried around to help.

"See what I mean? The kid's crazy. Now will you for Chrissake control him?"

Tommy let himself be dragged off the floor again and deposited beside me. I could feel him trembling. That instant he'd spent suspended in midair, staring down at the racing pavement, had drained the blood from his face and the strength from his angular body.

Returning to the front seat, Meadlow glanced over his shoulder. Unlike the pair of breathless, sweaty wrestlers in back, he was cool and dry and calm. "Listen, Tommy, I—"

"That's not my name."

"Yes, it is."

"No! I'm a born-again Christian and my new name is Tiagatha."

"I don't care if it's Hiawatha. What matters to me is that I'm responsible for you. Your parents asked me to talk to you."

"And deprogram me." The boy crossed his arms, hugging his chest as if he had a chill.

"And give you an opportunity to explain what you've been up to. Maybe you'll convert me."

"I know better than that."

"Then look at it as a chance to defend your faith. You've got nothing to be afraid of if you call on the Lord. Isn't that what the Bible says?"

The boy realized he was being led on and wouldn't answer.

"Well, isn't it?" Meadlow demanded. "Don't you believe the Bible? Doesn't it say the Lord is your shepherd and He'll protect you even in the valley of the shadow of death? Why be afraid of White Death?"

"Meadlow, you're going too far. Don't make fun."

"I'm not afraid of you," Tiagatha declared.

"Of course not. What's to be scared of? Now, settle down beside Padre Pio and think about what you're going to tell me."

"My name is Father Amico. Call me Tony if you like."

He called me nothing at all, and as the Chevy cruised around the unbanked curves of City Park Road, Tiagatha removed a miniature Bible from the holster he wore and read Scripture. At some passages he shut his eyes, silently mouthing the words.

When we swung onto Ranch Road 2222, there was a series of sharp explosions and the boy's eyes flipped open. At a skeet and rifle range, a posse of Department of Public Safety officers was firing at human silhouettes. Behind the targets, bullets and buckshot had torn through the trees, stripping them of leaves like locusts.

"Better go back to the Good Book," Meadlow said, "and study hard. I've read it a few times myself."

"Thaddeus warned me about you. I know the things you're capable of, but you can't hurt me. Not really. You could break all the bones in my body, but you can't rob me of God's grace."

"No one's going to break your bones," I said.

Tiagatha's eyes were incredulous now, rather than angry. "What kind of priest are you, anyway?"

"A Paulist father from St. Austin's parish. Your mother tells me you used to go there."

"You know that's not what I meant. What kind of priest would do a deprogramming?"

"I'm not doing it."

"But you're letting Meadlow do it. You're helping him when your vocation is to encourage Christian belief."

"I don't need anyone to tell me what my vocation is," I said, touchy as always on that topic.

"I think I'd rather deal with White Death. At least he won't kid me he's out to save my soul."

Meadlow laughed. "I'm after what's left of your brain."

"You don't understand my position," I said. "I'm here to help you."

But the boy returned to his Bible, and Meadlow laughed louder.

As we drove east, dropping down from the hills, my stomach experienced a sickening elevator dip. Then we entered a barren, bulldozed area where the trees and vegetation had been butchered and great patches of bare ground had been paved over with tract houses and asphalt.

Too many rats in a tight place produced frenzy, I had read. Someday they might run those tests on humans and discover that insanity is extrinsic—located in the landscape, not in the mind. The sight of an ugly intersection, for instance, snarled with traffic, blurred by exhaust fumes, might cause more problems than an Oedipus complex. The brain balked at it, just as the eye rebelled at certain color combinations and geometrical patterns, and if optical illusions led you to blink, maybe cerebral ones brought on breakdowns. Driving a freeway, as we were doing now, certainly had a deracinating effect on me.

But even as I entertained these possibilities, I knew I was fumbling for an excuse to avoid Tiagatha's question. What kind of priest was I?

South of Austin, I-35 sped us through an undulating countryside where the grass was scorched, the trees stunted, the leaves brown and curled like cigars. Cows huddled in the shade of gaudy billboards, chewing their cud and placidly watching cars zip past.

I looked forward to San Antonio as a break from my monotonous self-absorption, but Meadlow skirted it so that I saw only a few jagged brown teeth of the skyline and something called the Sanitary Tortilla Company. Outside the city limits, the land flattened and spread toward the hazy, heat-distorted horizon. A torrid wind, with nothing standing tall enough to stop it, skimmed up gravel and shot it, seething, against the sides of the Chevy, which shuddered as Meadlow fought to control it.

What little was left of the vegetation reminded me of the guts of a computer—all loose, waving wires and barbed transistors. Century plants jutted up like monstrous asparagus, and the mesquite and chaparral bushes wore garlands of trash. A few tumbleweeds whipped across the highway, while dust buzzed into the car through the cracks and the three of us coughed on the gritty air.

The drive gave me the giddy sensation of a fall. It seemed impossible for there to be so much space without a purpose, so much sand without a beach. Although I could peer ahead to where we would wind up half an hour from now, I could conceive of no reason to continue plummeting south to where the road narrowed to a pinpoint. Already I remembered Austin with longing, and decided Fr. Doyle hadn't misled me. It *was* Mecca compared to this Empty Quarter.

Evenly distanced on the endless stripe of pavement, the cars ahead of us appeared not to move at all, and I gauged our progress by the tiny towns that clung to the plumb-line straightness of the Interstate. In the off-light of the evening sun, yellowed by dust, Derby, Devine, Pearsall and Dilly were insects trapped in amber.

Meadlow left the highway at Encinal, a sorry cluster of houses surrounded by a faint grid of dirt roads. Still heading south, he followed the one paved street that ran parallel to the expressway, and several miles later, but just a few hundred yards from I-35, we came to the U-Et-Yet Cafe and Billie and Zack's Adobe Shacks.

The cafe was a large concrete box which, with half a dozen window air conditioners attached to it, appeared to have spawned smaller boxes. Behind it, the Adobe Shacks—white stucco, actually—lay scattered like bleached bones around a shimmering square of asphalt that might have been a poisoned waterhole. When Meadlow coasted across the parking lot, the tires hissed as if we'd hit a wet spot.

Aluminum awnings shaded each unit, and flowerpots swung from them by twine. A burly woman wearing a blue robe sat in front of shack number one, sipping a can of beer. She waved as we went by. Next to the shacks on the far side of the lot, other women, younger and slimmer, also lounged in the shade drinking.

Meadlow stopped at unit six. "Hold him while I unlock the door."

"Don't we have to check in?"

"That's taken care of. I rent a set of rooms here. But I haven't been back in a while, and I'd better look things over first."

Number six, unlike the other units, had an elaborate locking system. Pulling a key ring from his pocket, Meadlow unhooked the broad metal flange that fastened the door to the jamb, then inserted a second key in the knob. He stepped inside the shack and flicked on a light.

When he came back, he went around to the boy's side of the Chevy. "Okay, climb out nice and easy."

As I released him, Tiagatha holstered his Bible and slid toward Meadlow, stood up, stretched, and stamped his feet, which apparently had fallen asleep. Then he made a break for it, shouting, "Help! Help, I've been kidnapped!"

Pouncing like a puma, Meadlow nabbed him before he had gone five yards. They clawed and scratched at one another for a second, but the little man quickly gained the upper hand and the boy stopped struggling. Maybe he had noticed what I had —none of the women had stirred at his cries for help.

Meadlow lifted him bodily and lugged him into the room, saying in a perfectly level voice, "Don't do that again. I'm stronger than you, so why fight? And I'm much faster, so why waste your breath running?"

Stripped to the barest essentials, far more austere than my cell at St. Austin's, shack number six had a folding cot in the corner, two tubular chrome chairs with red Leatherette seats and backrests, and one bright bulb overhead. Nothing else. Masonite wallboard had been nailed over the windows to keep the daylight out and the deprogrammee in.

"How'd you ever find this motel?" I asked.

"I'm always on the lookout for cheap, private places to work. I've got setups like this in strategic spots across the country." He switched on the air conditioner, sat on one of the chairs and motioned the boy to the other.

"I'll stand," he said, nervously stroking his beard.

"No, sit down, Tommy."

"I told you, my name's Tiagatha."

"Suit yourself. Have a seat."

He sat down, clamping his hands to the sides of the chair as if he expected to be catapulted out of it, and started praying again, repeating the litany of chants and divine praises.

"Please stop that," Meadlow said mildly. Waspish in his attacks on me, he restrained himself with the boy. Even when he'd had to use force, he'd been careful not to harm him. "The sooner we start, the sooner we leave. If you don't like it here —and I appreciate how you wouldn't—why stay longer? Let's get on with it."

Tiagatha didn't appear to be listening. He chanted louder.

Crossing to the cot, I settled myself on its hard wooden edge. I was of two minds about this histrionic praying. Because of my own spiritual problems, part of me responded to the boy's devotion. But another part found it pointless and annoying. It seemed to squander precious energy, and I was impatient to hear what, if anything, Tiagatha had to say.

"I have all night," Meadlow said. "All this week and the next and the next. Believe me, you're going to talk sooner or later. Why not now, while we're in a good mood?"

Shutting his eyes, Tiagatha rocked and swayed as he chanted, and through the sparse strands of his hair I noticed perspiration bead on his scalp. It glistened in his beard, too, and spread dark semicircles under the arms of his shirt. Fright, exertion or fervor—something had slathered him with sweat, while Meadlow and I observed him from our dry, cool distance.

"You know, Tiagatha, this is why we're here in the first place. Your parents complain you won't talk, won't take the trouble to communicate. They accuse you of being a zombie. From what I've heard about Jesus, He wouldn't want you acting like that. According to the Bible, He didn't curl up in a shell. He moved around and spoke to the multitudes, bringing them the gospel. But how can you spread the word when you're mumbling to yourself? You're no Christian."

The boy opened his eyes.

"That's better. Why don't you tell us why you do this chanting?"

"Why should I? You talk about the Bible and Christ, but you don't believe." There was a quaver to his voice, and to stop shaking he held one hand in the other and pressed them both between his bony knees. In the raw light, his freckled complexion looked flecked with rust.

"That's a fact," Meadlow agreed. "I don't. But they say Jesus didn't turn His back on nonbelievers and sinners. When He was fasting forty days and forty nights in the wilderness, He even spoke to the devil. How do you get off acting so self-righteous? Are you holier than the Lord?"

"No."

"Then why do you shut yourself off by babbling?"

"I'm not babbling. I'm praying. Jesus instructed us to pray always, and He said, "I am the way, the truth, and the life; no man cometh unto the Father except—' "

"Hey, slow down. Don't jump ahead of yourself. Take a minute sometime and read Matthew 6, Verse 7. 'And in praying use not vain repetitions, as the Gentiles do: for they think that they shall be heard for their much speaking.' How does that grab you?"

By the nape of the neck, if one could judge by his expression. He seemed to be about to shut his eyes and start chanting again, but he said, "My prayers aren't in vain. I repeat them sincerely. God knows that because He's in my heart."

"Maybe. Maybe not. I just know what's in the Book." Meadlow leaned forward, planting his elbows on his knees. "How can you be so sure you're serving God by mumbling these jingles?"

"I won't stop praying."

"Not even when it puts you at odds with other people?"

" 'No man can serve two masters; for either he will hate the one and love the other; or else he will hold one, and despise the other. Ye cannot serve God and mammon.' "

"They've had you studying hard, no doubt about it. But nobody mentioned mammon and masters. We were speaking about human beings and how you isolate yourself. Seems to me if religion has any value there should be room for everybody. But you, you've excluded people and you've hurt them, especially your parents."

"They've hurt me more. I won't stay around and let them destroy my soul."

Meadlow shook his head sadly, his gestures and expressions as exaggerated as the boy's, and I began to suspect that Tiagatha hadn't revealed any more of his true feelings than Meadlow had. "You don't hesitate to throw the first stone, do you? Remember what the Bible warns about not judging others. And you might recall the Fourth Commandment, 'Honor thy father and thy mother.' "

"That depends on what you mean by 'honor.' There are other passages, you know. 'And everyone that hath left houses, or brethren, or sisters, or father, or mother, or children, or lands, for my name's sake shall receive a hundredfold, and shall inherit eternal life.' "

Meadlow shook his head once more. "What I don't understand is why God says honor them one minute and leave them the next. Why does He tell you to look after your family and your fellow man, then switch around and order you to abandon them and follow Him? It doesn't make sense."

Tiagatha was unperturbed. "Christ never promised an easy path or complete contentment in this life. He said, 'Do not imagine that I have come to bring peace to the earth; I have come to bring a sword, not peace. I have come to set a man apart from his father, and the daughter from her mother, and the daughter-in-law from her mother-in-law; a man's enemies shall be the people of his own house.' "

"Yes, I recognize the passage. Matthew 10:34–37. But don't

quit there. Skim on down to 26:51–53. 'Put your sword into your scabbard, for all those who take up the sword will perish by the sword.' How is that? You can't have it both ways." Meadlow pitched to his feet, prowling. "For every passage you quote, I'll cite one that contradicts it and condemns you. Let's face it, Tiagatha. You ought to find something better than the Bible to depend on, because the Good Book is a lot of double-talking gobbledegook."

"Don't say that! It's the word of God."

"Then draw your own conclusion. His word is double-talk." He was stalking Tiagatha, circling in for the kill. "If you like to believe in God, that's your business. But be honest and admit the Bible is bullshit."

"Knock that off," I said.

"You stay out of this."

"I won't stand for that sort of talk." But having hoped for more than a clash of Biblical quotations, I was irritated as much by the boy's feeble answers as by Meadlow's blasphemy.

"You're interrupting me."

"Too bad. Watch your mouth."

"I'll deal with you later." Meadlow turned back to Tiagatha, but the boy was gone. Closing his eyes, he had leaned forward in the chair crooning. "See what you did?" the little man lashed at me. "You let him off the hook just when he was about to break." He shook Tiagatha by the shoulders. "Okay, cut it out. We've been through this. That's not prayer. That doesn't please God."

"How do you know?" I asked.

"I told you to butt out."

"And I told you I won't. Talk to him all you want. But don't presume to tell him what prayer is or what pleases God. You don't know."

"He's right," Meadlow said, swiftly changing tactics. "You don't know what God wants, Tiagatha. Not even a priest does."

"That's not what I said."

"You live in darkness, a victim of wild guesses. What kind of life is that? You've got the intelligence to make better choices. Use your brain, and stay open to the truth."

"Praise the Lord praise the Lord praise Jesus. PraisetheLord-praisetheLordpraisetheLordpraiseJesus." As the boy's breathing quickened, his face flushed and his prayers gathered intensity.

Meadlow clutched his arm as if to save a swimmer about to go under for good. "Open your eyes. Darkness doesn't help. Talk to us."

Tiagatha's lips and tongue fluttered in a shrill ululating cry while his feet tapped time on the floor and his arms and upper body trembled. Though the sounds didn't make sense to me, they seemed to have the coherency of language, a shape and secret meaning the boy comprehended. Or was he suffering from a seizure?

"Dammit, don't do this," Meadlow shouted. "You're not spiting me. You're hurting yourself by hiding from the truth."

"Leave him alone. Maybe he's an epileptic." I hastened to his side, studying his face. The eerie expression, a mixture of exaltation and agony, unsettled me. I touched him, as the deprogrammer had, yet wasn't sure I had made contact. "Are you okay?" I asked.

"For Chrissake, don't encourage him. I checked his medical record. There's nothing wrong with him. He'd like us to think he's speaking in tongues. Listen to that horseshit." He yelled in Tiagatha's face, "It won't work, I'm warning you! You can't keep this up forever. When you run out of breath, I'll be right here, ready to start all over."

Brushing aside my hand, the boy bounded to his feet and shimmied in place, muttering and making wide welcoming gestures with his arms.

"We ought to get help," I said. "There's something wrong

with him. One of these little towns must have a doctor."

"I tell you he's not sick. He's *inspired.* He feels praise and the anointing of the spirit. Jesus has entered his heart, and he's been filled. Now he's dancing in the spirit. Listen close and you'll hear his prophecy. Christ, what a clown show you people encourage. The best cure for this kid would be a swift kick in the ass."

But Meadlow deferred that form of direct therapy and began to bellow and yodel himself. Pinwheeling his arms, he skipped circles around the boy, a grotesque parody of a man possessed.

"Look, Tiagatha, you did it. You converted me. I've got the feeling, I've got the gift of prophecy, and it tells me you're full of shit. Or, in your language, 'Yooyooyayowyowlalladeela.' "

I had to flee before I, too, started shaking and screaming, not in a swoon of ecstasy or illumination, but in stark fear of the irrational. I stepped outside, leaned against the stucco wall and let the warm air wash over me.

Though in my own worst moments I had become as immobile as stone, Tiagatha somehow reminded me of myself, my former self, that shambling silent creature they had shipped off to Rome. I had escaped him on the psychiatrist's couch, I hoped, and I was now almost as eager to escape this boy, allow the deprogrammer to do his job, and be done with it.

Yet even with a wall between me and that demented dervishing, I felt threatened. Glossolalia is what they called it. Commonly known as speaking in tongues. Supposedly it bestowed upon people the ability, not to predict the future, but to speak the truth in God's name.

I resisted the notion. No, I more than resisted it. I feared it and was ashamed of myself. While it was true that like most men I couldn't stand very much reality, I seemed to have a limited taste for wonderment as well. Perhaps Tiagatha had spoken the only truth available to him. "Yooyooyayowyowlalladeela." But that wasn't the answer I needed.

Pushing away from the wall, I went to collect my luggage from the car. Except for an old pickup truck and Meadlow's Chevy, the parking lot was empty. The women had disappeared indoors, and a few flickering bats dive-bombed at insects in the semi-darkness. While a breeze blew out of the south, its sound the distillation of loneliness, I risked one look at the surrounding desolation, at the sky striped purple and red and gold like various paths to heaven—or in this case, toward California—then hurried into room five.

I couldn't say what kind of clientele Billie and Zack's Adobe Shacks normally catered to, but every article of furniture had been chained to the floor. That called for a lot of chain, since the room was cluttered by a double bed, two night tables with blue gooseneck lamps, two Leatherette chairs, a combination chest of drawers–desk–vanity table and mirror, and a color television. Though I detested TV in principle, I flicked the set on when I passed it, eager for company if not for conversation.

I was hungry and had been for hours, but since I didn't care to face whoever or whatever might be at the U-Et-Yet Cafe, I peeled off my sweat-dampened clothes and decided to take a shower. As I walked to the bathroom, several puckered squares of tile snapped down, then popped up. A lizard with a flashing tail—a gecko, I guessed—raced from behind the toilet and up the wall. I let it alone. It'll eat insects, I thought. Everything eats something.

Water shot from the shower head in a single thick jet that smelled strongly of sulfur. I might as well have been bathing in rotten eggs, and the idea of drinking it was unbearable, but it refreshed me for a few minutes.

Then, as soon as I dried off and dressed, I began to wilt again. The windows were nailed shut, and I didn't like leaving the door open to strange insects and stranger eyes. Because it seemed better to freeze than to suffocate, I switched on the air conditioner and sagged onto the bed, which sagged in turn, rolling me to a soft spot at its center. I shut my eyes an instant, but since that rendered me vulnerable to thoughts of the boy and doubts about myself, I tried to concentrate on the TV. What I didn't want was to ask myself what I was doing here in this improbable place with these impossible people, for I feared that would lead to still more futile questions.

My psychiatrists had repeatedly asked why I had become a priest, and I had answered, "Because I believe in God, and that seemed the way to serve him. That's the best reason I can offer." But they weren't satisfied with the best reason, and so, summoning up memories of childhood, I admitted to other motives. I loved the smell of beeswax and altar wine, of incense and sacred oils. I thrilled to the sound of Latin and Gregorian chant and organ music, even as played by the heavy-pedaling Mr. Snyder in our parish. While most boys crowded the basketball court, I came to the church, which was dim and quiet and private, unlike our apartment, which was bright with naked light bulbs, cacophonous with children, visiting relatives and friends. Though at home there was also the smell of bread and wine, there was no place to think or to pray, and as a child I believed that the job of a priest was to spread the orderly silence of the church throughout the parish.

Of course, as it turned out, things had thundered in the opposite direction. The world crashed through the quiet of the Church like a tidal wave, marooning many of us on distant spits of land.

Someone knocked at the door, and before I could speak, Meadlow came in, carrying a plastic tray. "Mind if I sit down?" he asked with unusual diffidence.

I answered with a shrug.

He went to the far side of the double bed and set the tray between us. "You hungry? I brought something to eat."

"Maybe in a minute." I meant to ignore the tray, the little man and his unexpected kindness, but I couldn't stop breathing, couldn't help smelling deep-fat fried food. From the corner of my eye I caught sight of a greasy envelope stuffed with shoestring potatoes, a tall Dixie cup of Coke and two bulging objects wrapped in aluminum foil. FLAME-KISSED BURGERS FROM OUR SIZZLE KITCHEN was stenciled in red letters on top. "Has the boy eaten?" I asked, holding back.

"I took him a tray."

"But did he eat?"

"I didn't wait around to watch. He won't eat in front of me. They're all like that. They think they're punishing me. He'll dig in when he's hungry."

"How was he when you left?"

"Quiet, tired. He didn't have the energy to go on with his act. It's usually that way. Subconsciously most of them want to be deprogrammed."

"I don't know. He seemed pretty set in his beliefs."

"They all do in the beginning. But take it from me, the ones who put up the stiffest early resistance are the easiest to break."

"What if they don't break?"

"Then you've got a job on your hands, a real challenge. I enjoy it and just take it in stages."

"What stages?" Under cover of his answer, I reached for a few shoestring potatoes and one of the "flame-kissed" burgers, which was impossible to unwrap quietly.

Meadlow interrupted himself to say, "Eat them both if you like."

"What about you?"

"I don't have any appetite." He sipped from a quart bottle of soda. "Never do when I'm working."

"Why the soda?"

"A nervous stomach. Gas starts backing up on me when I don't get enough exercise."

"Sure you don't want this?" I slipped the second burger onto my lap.

"Positive." He had his eyes on the TV, and smiled at something. "Ever catch this show? It's kind of clever."

"I don't watch much television. I've never liked it."

"Don't like it?" He sounded personally offended.

"It's not this particular show I'm against." I was nibbling another potato. "I'm opposed to TV in general because of the lousy programs and the way it's wrecked so many marriages. I hear in the confessional all the time how it causes family fights and has killed off the art of conversation."

"Hell, that's an art that was practiced at such a low level for so many centuries it deserved to die. If TV killed off anything, it was the art of crocheting or staring at blank walls. Face it, most people are dumb and dull and don't know what to do with themselves. But that little machine is a lot more interesting than your average human being. More efficient, too."

"That's a frightening thought," I said, side-stepping the full impact of it by biting into a burger.

"Frightening or not, it's the truth. If it weren't, you'd hire a person to stand over there and talk. But you've got a TV."

"It's not mine."

"You turned it on." His voice had assumed its familiar cutting edge, and I was appalled to think that after a long afternoon of verbal sparring he was ready for another round.

"You were telling me about the stages of a deprogramming. Where do you go from here? From what I heard, Tiagatha should be hard to talk to, hard to reach."

"No, I got to him a few times already. You have to learn what to look for. It's like in boxing when you tag a guy. He'll cover up, pretend he's not hurt. But you see the shock in his eyes."

"I didn't notice Tiagatha's eyes. He had them shut most of the time."

"Don't you worry. I made contact, and I'll roust him out of his shell before long. It's just a matter of jabbing away until he drops his guard. I'll make him ashamed to fall back on chanting and talking in tongues. Then I'll tell him if he has the courage of his convictions, he won't depend on the Bible. Then I'll start in—"

"On God?"

Meadlow chuckled. "No need for that. If you kill the body, the head dies, too."

Suddenly the meat had a tainted taste. I put aside the burger and pushed the tray toward him. "That must give you a lot of satisfaction."

He suppressed a soda belch. "You bet it does."

"Seems to me you could get your kicks some other way."

"I get mine by performing a valuable service to the individual and to society. How do you get yours, Padre?"

"I haven't had many lately. I suppose you believe you're doing these kids a big favor, and you're dead set on doing it whether they want it or not."

"Who cares what they want?"

"That's an awful thing to say."

"Why? The Catholic Church has always forced people to do what they didn't want. When you had the muscle, you used it. Remember the Inquisition? You tortured and killed people—all for their own good, of course, all to save souls. Well, I don't give a damn about souls. I'm out to shape up their lives."

"Fine. And good luck to you. But how does that justify trying to destroy their faith?"

"Simple. You can't improve someone's life if it's based on illusions." Soda bottle in hand, he stood up and paced the room. "It's not just God I'm against. It's all the bullshit people believe in—kooky politics, soft-minded psychology, nutrition fads. But religion is the worst. When you hear a man say he believes in God, you've got a man you can't count on. It's not necessarily that he'll lie to you, but he believes in lies and that can be worse. That's the reason the world's in such a mess."

"Why blame it all on religion, Meadlow? Most people don't care about it one way or the other."

"You're wrong. Pick up any rock and watch what comes

crawling out—hundreds and thousands of closest Catholics, Protestants and Jews. In a crunch, they run right back to God. In my business the hardest part is spotting the secret believers before they have a chance to do damage."

I sighed. "Look, I just don't understand what you hope to gain. Let's say you badger this boy out of his beliefs, what'll that accomplish?"

"It'll show what I could do if I had more support. Right now, I'm restricted by petty, short-sighted authorities who'll let me work on one weirdo in a motel room but who draw the line at anything meaningful. Hell, half the time I'm fighting with one hand tied behind me, but I figure whenever I break a Jesus Freak it proves what I could do if I dropped the kid gloves. We have statistics that indicate if we applied our experiments across the board, operating under the correct controls and reinforcements, we could—"

"All right, already. It's late, Meadlow. I'm tired of talking."

"You're too lazy to think." He stopped at the foot of the bed and glared down his snip of a nose. "Your brain is as blubbery as your body. Don't you realize, reason would work if we gave it a chance?"

"Maybe religion would, too. The point is, people won't give you a chance. It's not in their nature."

"Their nature is what the conditions dictate. I did a print-out on this."

Sighing again, I waved a weary hand. "Why not forget computers for once and deal with people directly?"

"Personalities foul up the equation. They're messy and inefficient."

"That pretty well describes most people I've met, myself included. Which raises the question, How are all these messy, inefficient folks supposed to operate your flawless system?"

He pulled himself up to his full height, jammed his fists into his pockets and jangled his keys. "I see there's no sense discussing this."

"Probably not. Life's too short to waste time talking about print-outs."

Meadlow set his jaw as he muttered, "Yes, it is short and I've got better things to do than shoot the breeze with you." He ripped open the door and stalked off toward his room.

As I went over to lock up behind him, several cars swept onto the lot and parked next to the shacks where the girls had been sitting. I heard music and laughter from that direction, and an arid wind whining against the windows and walls.

Clearing the tray of food from my bed, I laid it on the floor beside the door. The television was broadcasting the late news in Spanish when I snapped it off and undressed. Then I hit the light switch, reducing the room to darkness laced with the aroma of French fries and congealing hamburger.

The idea of praying flickered through my muddled thoughts like one of those bats dive-bombing the insects outside, but I remained motionless until the urge passed. After a day of fending off a deprogrammer and a Jesus Freak, I had nothing more to say to anyone.

V

I stepped out of the room and into an oven. The sun was bright and hot enough to burn holes in my eyeballs. Glancing off to one side, toward the battered pickup beside Meadlow's Chevy, I noticed on the flat-bed what appeared to be a rusty crucifix rising above a clutter of junk. Certain it had to be a mirage, I moved from under the awning for a closer look. Spears of heat pierced every inch of my exposed skin as I squinted and satisfied myself it was a tire iron standing in a coil of greasy rope.

Next to unit number seven a clump of green weeds flourished on the moisture that fell drop by drop from the throbbing air conditioner, and Meadlow crouched there, rooting around, searching for something. I went and stood behind him. I wanted to ask whether he had gotten any sleep last night when cars had come and gone at all hours, spinning their tires and unspooling the harsh racket of their horns. Just before dawn, somebody had chucked a beer can against my door, and I had been awake ever since. Now the parking lot was almost empty, baking in the morning sun, and the pickup and the Chevy, their headlights splattered with bugs, looked as bleary-eyed as I felt.

The little man straightened up and turned around. It wasn't

Meadlow. Older and not nearly as muscular, this fellow nevertheless acted spry and fearless as a sparrow. Pushing past me, he said, "Hi! How are you all?" Then he flung out his arm, flicking a grey blob from his index finger onto the parking lot. A slug wormed its way into shape and, waving stubby antennae, oozed across the macadam, shriveling as it proceeded, depositing a glistening trail of its own guts.

The man smiled, and his wisp of a mustache wriggled like the slug. "Look at that. In a minute there won't be nothing left except one long pecker track." He wiped his hand cursorily on his hip and held it out for me to shake. "Zack Horskus. You here with Meadlow?"

"Yes."

"Well, you're welcome anyhow. Anybody might could have an asshole for a friend. How long you plan to stay?"

"I don't know. Meadlow's not my friend. I'm just . . . Is it always this hot?" I retreated under an awning.

"Hell, no," he said, joining me. "Sometimes it's hotter. Then, on the other hand, in winter there'll blow a blue norther and it'll be colder than a well-digger's butt. Couple, three years back I wore terminal underwear all during December, January and February. Makes you wonder why anybody'd live in this shithole."

"I gather you're not from here."

"You gather right. I was originally born in Oklahoma. Broken Bow."

"That's different, I suppose."

"You bet your sweet ass it is. For one thing, business is booming up there what with all those oil roughies running around with money in their jeans."

"I see," I said, fumbling for the words to soothe Zack's sizzling temper. "Maybe you'll move back someday."

"No way, no how. I'll be stuck here till they put me in a box and plant it. Who'd be dumb enough to buy us out? I was stupid to set up this far south. But I shouldn't bitch about it. That's all behind me now. When you're young, you make mistakes. You know how it is."

I nodded that I did.

"Hell, back then I didn't have no more brains than a doodlebug. I always followed the line that it was smart to invest my money in houses and lots."

"I guess real estate is a risky business."

"Shit on real estate. I'm talking about whorehouses and lots of whiskey." Elbowing me in the belly, Zack tossed his head and laughed. Damp grey streamers of hair unfurled, then fell into place.

I smiled weakly. Somehow I seemed to be missing significant transitions. "You do own quite a piece of property."

"Who you kidding?" he asked, angry again.

"Well, it's convenient to the highway."

"Don't talk to me about that road. That's what near killed us. There's no turnoff, so how the hell are customers supposed to get over here? Tourists buzz on by us and down to Laredo. We were a hundred yards closer and the bastards would've had to buy us out. But they just left us stewing in our juice. You seen them signs at interstate motels, 'Easy-Off, Easy-On'? Well, I built one said 'Hard-Off, Hard-On,' but the Highway Department made me tear it down. Who are they to blame us no matter what we do?"

"I don't blame you a bit. I see why you're upset."

"See?" Zack narrowed his eyes as if I'd called his vision into question. "Hell, you haven't seen the half of it. You got any idea how boresome it is here, not to mention the bad business?"

"I can imagine."

"Not now, you can't. But wait a couple, three days, then you'll know what lonesome is. There ain't nothing or nobody in Encinal, and what with the cost of gas, Laredo's too far to communicate to except once a week."

I pretended to survey the road. "Maybe they'll build a turn-off soon. It's a likely spot."

"I ain't even hoping for that. I just wish they'd condemn us and pay for the property." He hocked and spat an oyster toward the parking lot. It evaporated the instant it hit the asphalt. " 'Course, the place ain't really worth a bucket of warm spit. It's every bit of it nothing but Saturday night land."

"Come again?" I cocked my head, tilting an ear closer to Zack.

"Saturday night land's what the Lord made at the last minute after working all week to fix those folks up North some good property. By the time He got down here, He'd shot His wad and was going through the motions, waiting to pack it in and catch Him a day's rest."

"I wish I could help you," I mumbled. "Have you seen Meadlow this morning?"

"Yeah, he et breakfast early and headed off that-away." Zack pointed beyond the parking lot to the fields of sage and mesquite.

"Where was he going?"

"Beats me. He was in his underwear."

"There must be some mistake."

"He made it. Not me."

"Was he alone? Did he have a bearded boy with him?"

"Nope. The hippie's locked in his room."

"Has the boy had breakfast?"

"Yeah. Meadlow brung it to him. How about you? You et yet?"

"No, I haven't." And I felt woozy from hunger, or the heat, or Zack.

"Come on over to the cafe"—he said it so it rhymed with safe—"and dig into a plate of hot kikes."

"Pardon?" How many times could I ask him to repeat himself before he decided I was deaf or brain-damaged?

"Hot kikes and syrup and sausage. Come on."

As we passed under the other awnings, which shimmered like cookie sheets, Zack asked, "What are you, anyway? Same thing as Meadlow?"

"No, I'm a priest."

"No shit. What kind?"

"Paulist."

"I mean American or Mexican?"

"American. I'm from New York."

"Yeah, I reckon that explains how you look and talk and all. What are you doing hanging around Meadlow?"

"I'm here to provide a Catholic influence for the deprogramming."

"The what?"

"Don't you know what Meadlow does?"

"He told us he tracks down runaways—hippies, mostly—and fetches them here for a good talking to before he carries them home."

"That's partly true. But he also—"

"Stop right there." Zack flourished his callused palm like a traffic cop. "I'd as soon not know what happens in any of these rooms. People pay the rent, that's good enough for me."

In front of unit number one the burly woman in the blue velour robe lounged under the awning. From a distance I had known she was big, but only as we approached could I appreciate exactly how huge she was.

"Hey, Billie," Zack called. "We got a priest bunking here."

"You don't say." She eyed me over the rim of a beer can as she tilted it and took a sip of Pearl. Around her wrist and elbow there were deep creases in the flesh as if the sections of her arm had been screwed into place. "Those nuns must feed you real good. You're pretty near as big as me."

But that was flattery or effrontery, because nobody was anywhere near as big as Billie. She had expanded in all directions until she resembled a great fortress of fat. A brier patch of grey wires bristled from her scalp, and her upper lip had sprouted a dark line of down, the blueprint for a mustache like her husband's. Beneath the robe, her legs—hairy purple-veined pillars—barely slimmed at her ankles. She wore high-top black gym shoes slit at the sides to relieve her bunions, and these, along with the robe, lent her the look of a heavyweight wrestler.

"What's your name, anyway?" Zack asked.

"Anthony Amico. Call me Tony."

"But he's from New York, not Mexico."

"You speak any Spanish?" Billie asked.

"No, I'm Italian. That is, my parents were."

"Too bad. Thought you might could talk to this new boy we got working for us. He doesn't speak a word of English."

"Maybe Tony could talk Italian to Chiquita Banana. That boy wouldn't notice the difference."

"Zack, every time you open your mouth you make about as much sense as a fart." She held the beer can toward me. "Like a cold brew?"

"No, thanks. I haven't eaten breakfast yet."

"When you're ready for one, just holler. We have a whole fridge full. It's the only way to fly in this weather." Fishing around behind her feet, Billie pulled up what looked like a shiny toy tank and plopped it onto her lap. It was a baby armadillo on a leash, one end of which had been hooked to the leg of the chair. At the other end, a dog collar had been buckled around the animal's armor-plated midsection.

"You decide yet whether it's a Mary or a Mike?" Zack asked.

"It's a Mike, all right. I noticed the other night he's growing a teeny little dingle. You like him?" she asked me.

"Very interesting."

"Here, want to hold him?"

"No, thanks. I haven't eaten yet."

Billie cuddled it close to her face and cooed, "They're so cute and lovable when they're this size, it purely tears me up to think of killing them later."

"You kill them? Why?"

"Flowerpots."

"Do they knock them over or eat the flowers or what?"

Billie coughed up a seismic burst of laughter. "Hell, no. I raise them to make flowerpots out of their shells." She showed me a deep-dish scaly shell that swung from the awning by three lengths of twine and was overgrown with bougainvillaea.

"Very nice. I'd better go look for Meadlow," I said. "He's probably wondering where I am."

"Oh, he ran off an hour ago. In his long johns." She waved the way Zack had, off toward the stunted thicket of sage and mesquite that undulated in the morning heat as if it was being consumed by a smokeless fire.

"I'll wait for him in the restaurant. Good to meet you."

But before I could escape, a skinny, sick-looking Mexican boy stepped out of room number one, pushing a cart cluttered with brooms, mops, brushes and bottles of cleanser and disinfectant.

"Chiquita Banana," Billie called to him, and he shyly said, "*Terminado.*" His dark eyes, already large, appeared bigger yet because of the blue ovals under them. For some reason he fastened them upon me. Apparently he hadn't slept well, either—not just last night, but for months. Beneath a superficial tan, his face had a waxy pallor, his lips a bluish undertone. He wiped his hands on his uniform, which had once been white but now bore a crazy-quilt pattern of palm and fingerprints. Billie said it looked like a pack of monkeys had been climbing up and down him.

Zack started telling the boy what to do next, acting out his instructions. "*Ahora,* snatch the turkey and brush the rink. Brush, brush." He swayed in a wide sweeping motion. "In *todas las cameras. Todas.* And bounce the bundles, slick down the sleets and puff up the marshmallows." He scurried around Billie as though she were a king-size bed he was making up, and while he smoothed the blue velour over her varicose thighs and took phantom passes at her pillowed breasts, she winked at me and could scarcely contain her laughter. "Then dip into the dumper and squeegee, squeegee, squeegee." He rotated his arms, a man churning butter. "Use *mucho* bubbly. *Mucho.* Then flush the toy-toy."

Still staring at me, the boy muttered, "*Sí,*" and hauled his heavy cart to the next shack.

"You think he understood?" I asked.

"Who knows?" Billie said. "Last week he left the bottom sheets off the beds. This week he's liable to spread the rubber mats on top."

"You go through this every morning?"

"Oh, I don't mind," Zack said, patting his face with a wad of Kleenex. "Matter of fact, I enjoy it. But before long he'll remember what-all he has to do. Lazy and fruity as he acts, he ain't dumb."

"Maybe he'd learn English quicker if you spoke slower and used the right words."

"Man, you're missing the point by a mile." Billie emptied her can and crushed it.

"That's what we don't want," Zack said. "Soon as he knows English, he'll right away ask for more money. Or else head north and land a better job. We do what we can to hang on to our help, or to fix their asses if they run off on us. We had one boy a while back, really bright, a regular Paul Parrot. He picked up every word you said, so I was super careful around him. But he got to feeling cocky anyway, cut out on us, hitch-hiked up to Dallas, stopped at the first motel he seen and said, 'Welcome, I will be your dog. I can cook, crap and diddle a garbage can.' "

As the Horskuses broke into laughter, the risible mood seized Billie by sections, rippling from the buttress of her breasts along the shelf of her shoulders, down the struts of her arms and into her dowel-thick fingers. Zack hopped from foot to foot, tickled to the soles of his shoes.

When they recovered, I said, "I'd better get some breakfast."

"Good idea," Zack said. "I'm with you. Like to tag along, Billie?"

"Naw, I'll stick to Pearl."

The U-Et-Yet Cafe had the hectic clattering atmosphere of a communal kitchen. About a dozen people bustled around inside, all of them with free rein of the place so that it was impossible to separate the customers from the employees. Six or seven of them, men and women both, none in uniform, clustered behind the hissing grill, bumped hips and giggled as they fried up batches of potatoes, eggs, bacon and sausage. I thought I recognized a few of the girls who had been sitting in the shade of the adobe shacks the night before, but nobody took special notice of me or Zack.

He had vainly hollered out our order several times before a buxom woman with hair like a silver helmet came in the cafe door behind us. Hooking his arm through hers, he swung her around in a square-dance step. "Hey, Cindy, how about rustling us up some sausages and hot kikes?"

She smiled, said "Shit, why'd you pick on me for?" and sauntered behind the grill. On the left buttock of her short shorts a blue patch read, DOWN WITH HOT PANTS.

"Shouldn't be long now," Zack assured me.

"Could we please sit down?" I said, feeling light-headed.

"Sure thing."

We found a booth beside a window with a view of the parking lot and the plains beyond. A combination of glare and agoraphobia forced me to turn aside in time to see a cowboy remove his straw hat, dunk a comb into his water glass and slick back his hair. My empty belly rumbled, but my appetite was waning.

Zack, playing a tinny rhythm with a fork against the Formica, raised his head and sniffed. "Smell them?"

I assumed he meant the hot cakes, and nodded that I did. The old man's energy, like Meadlow's, overwhelmed me, yet obviously that's what you needed to survive here—energy and endurance and the dumb desire to continue sucking in the scalding air, shoving one foot after the other through the dust.

"How long you known Meadlow?" Zack asked. "He's been here half a dozen times, but never more than a day or so, and me and Billie can't figure where he gets his cash."

As I was about to answer, the girl in hot pants brought our plates of sausages and syrupy pancakes, and he said, "Don't let anyone tell you they ain't healthy. How could some old sawdust cereal or sour great fruit be better for you?" Then, after the first bite, he jabbed his dripping fork over my shoulder. "Speaking of the devil, here's your buddy. Still in his underwear."

Emerging from a heat mirage, Meadlow jogged a zigzag path through the scrub brush and cactus, pumping his chunky arms and legs. Of course, he wasn't in his underwear. He wore the kind of outfit favored by men who dive headfirst from airplanes or into deep water. The orange elasticized silk clung like a glistening second skin, and as he raced onto the parking lot Billie set aside her beer can and sat up in the chair. The Mexican boy moved to the doorway of my room, watching the deprogrammer drive himself around and around the asphalt in a final burst of speed.

The owners of this threadbare motel might have done well to take his tightly knit physique as a model. And maybe Meadlow meant for them to do just that. Maybe he intended to set a fast pace and a fine example and rescue the entire human race from its seedy disrepair.

But Zack laughed out loud. "Look at that little tit-head. Who'd work up a sweat on a day like this?"

* * *

When I left the cafe and crossed the lot, the deprogrammer was sitting outside Tiagatha's room, freshly shaved, showered and dressed in his quasi-clerical street clothes. His eyes were shut, his lips silently moving.

"Saying your morning prayers?" I asked, still probing for a tender spot.

"Quiet. I'm concentrating."

"On what?"

Meadlow opened his eyes. "You just won't quit bugging me, will you?"

"I'm curious. What are you up to?"

"I'm preparing myself. Jesus Freaks are pretty predictable, and these deprogrammings tend to follow a pattern. I hear the same answers, the same objections, the same silly ploys. So I stay a step ahead of them and have one or two responses ready for whatever they say."

"Sounds to me like the boy isn't the only one who's predictable. It's strange you have to program yourself before you deprogram him. Is your heart really in this?"

"My heart has nothing to do with it. Neither do any of the other nitwit excuses you use to avoid thinking." He climbed to his feet. "Where were you this morning? Thought you were going to start simulated Marine Corps training and get rid of that gut."

"Maybe tomorrow."

Meadlow unlocked the metal flange, smiling. "What is it they claim the road to hell is paved with?" Without waiting for an answer, he shoved the door wide.

Tiagatha sat in a chair, his lips pressed to a thin, straight line. His beard was tangled and his sparse sandy hair stood up in tufts as if he had spent the night yanking at it.

"Here we are," Meadlow sang brightly, sitting in front of him. Their knees nearly touched. "How are you?"

The boy didn't answer, and when I said, "Good morning,"

he ignored me, too. I sat on the sagging canvas cot and leaned against the wall.

"Why aren't you chanting?" Meadlow asked. "We might as well get that out of the way."

Tiagatha folded his arms.

"Don't let me interfere," said the little man. "Cut loose and wail."

"How much longer are you going to hold me?" Tiagatha asked.

"How long is a piece of string?"

"I want to know."

"So do I," Meadlow said, "but I don't. The one thing I'm positive of is that we'll stay put until you start talking sense."

" 'Sense' according to your definition."

"No, 'sense' according to the best definition."

"At least let me call Thaddeus and tell him I'm all right."

"No dice."

The boy shook his head, whipping his hair from side to side, but the rest of him was rigid as if we had tied him to the chair. "You won't brainwash me no matter how long you keep me."

"Brainwash? Who said anything about brainwashing?" Meadlow appealed to me as an arbiter.

The boy seemed to appeal to me, too. "Nobody's going to hurt you," I said. "We're here to talk."

"Exactly," the deprogrammer said, "and all I demand is that you be reasonable."

"What gives you the right to demand anything from me?"

Meadlow arched his faint eyebrows. "You will grant that I have a right to ask you to be reasonable?"

"I know what you mean by reasonable, and I have a right to be anything I want, even unreasonable, as long as I'm not hurting anybody."

"But you're hurting yourself. You're hurting your parents."

Again Tiagatha glanced at me, the weak link. "This is illegal. Don't you realize that?"

"He doesn't realize any such thing," Meadlow said. "The police know what we're doing."

"Does that make it right?"

"Whatever else it does, it makes your question irrelevant."

"You mean you can kidnap me and lock me up and—"

"Look," Meadlow said, "if you have any objections, wait till this's over and take legal action. But I'm warning you, you'll be wasting your time."

"Since you're so sure of that, let me call a lawyer now."

When the boy stood up, the little man forced him back into the chair. "I said later. After we're finished."

"Are you going to let him get away with this?" Tiagatha asked me.

"He doesn't have any choice." From Meadlow's tone, I knew he was speaking to me as well as to Tiagatha.

The boy pleaded with me. "Don't you see? It's me today, but it could be you tomorrow. Pentecostal groups are helpless because nobody'll protect us. But what happens if the Catholic Church loses its power?"

"The way you act, you don't deserve protection," Meadlow said. "Sympathy maybe, but not coddling. What you need is education and rehabilitation."

"He calls it rehabilitation, but it's persecution, pure and simple. Why won't you help me?"

My back, pressed to the wall, had begun to perspire despite the air conditioning, and as the two of them hung on my answer I felt I was hanging like a trapeze artist between them. "You heard what he said. What choice do I have?"

"What would you do if I was still a Catholic? What if he kidnapped a priest and told him to deny the Trinity or threatened to hold him until he stopped believing in the Transubstantiation?"

"Yeah, Padre, what would you do?" Now Meadlow folded his arms. "Or don't you care about that stuff any more?"

"Of course I do. But that's not the issue."

"I think it is," Meadlow said.

"I *know* it is," Tiagatha said as anger pumped color to his scalp. "Any normal priest would realize it's important to support other believers, no matter what their religion. Don't you have any backbone?"

"Please. You're getting angry and overwrought."

"Wouldn't you, if he was holding you prisoner?"

"And I think it's this overreaction that your parents are worried about. You don't have to act like a fanatic to convince me—much less God—of your faith."

"I'm not a fanatic. If my actions seem extreme, it's only because Meadlow's are. That's his trick. He uses his fanaticism to force you into a position that looks fanatical, too."

"You haven't seen me chanting and wearing a beard and living with a lot of creeps in a commune," Meadlow said.

"Why does it matter how I dress or talk or act? I know you disagree with me. I know you don't want to live like me. But why drag me here this way?"

"Because you've upset your parents and wasted your education and thrown away your family's money."

"Even so, even if that was true . . ." He shouted to silence the deprogrammer, then spoke more softly. "Why me? Of all the unusual life styles today, why pick on Pentecostal groups?"

"You gotta start somewhere," said Meadlow.

"But he wouldn't dare abduct an Orthodox Jew or a Black Muslim. They're too powerful. And he wouldn't grab a dope pusher or a pornographer and deprogram him. But he'll torment me because no one cares about unconventional Christians." Tiagatha was speaking directly to me. "Sooner or later, he'll come after you, too. Then you'll know what it means to have to defend yourself, to act like a fanatic to preserve your faith. Why wait until then? Why not help me now?"

"I . . . uh, look, you don't need my help. You seem quite capable of defending yourself. The way you're talking, you could easily answer Meadlow's questions and explain things to your parents, and we'd get this over with today."

"That's right, Tiagatha." Meadlow was maneuvering himself between the boy and me. "Let's finish this and get out of here."

"You're on his side, aren't you?"

"Not at all. I just believe you could explain your position to your parents if you stayed calm. If you like, I'll go along and stand by you."

"I don't need you to stand by me. Why don't we stand *up* to him? There are two of us."

Meadlow laughed and unfolded his arms. "Hope you boys are wearing your jockstraps."

"Don't do anything crazy," I begged the boy. "Think how much simpler it would be to go to your parents and talk things over."

Tiagatha's arms slipped apart and his hands fell palms up on his lap. "There's nothing to explain. Nothing I haven't said before. They know what I believe. I guess that's why I'm here."

"You're here because they're concerned," Meadlow said. "You've been acting illogical and inconsistent, and don't recognize it. Like you claim to be a Christian, but do you love your parents?"

"I don't want to talk about my family."

"Why not? They talk about you."

"I can imagine what they say."

"They say they love you and care for you."

"They have a strange way of showing it."

"It's not strange at all. They're trying to help. They know people are taking advantage of you and they'd like to give you back your brain."

"There's nothing the matter with my brain. They ought to worry about their own. And their souls. Tell them to leave me alone. That's how they can help."

"You couldn't expect them to do that. Not after what you've done."

"I haven't done anything wrong," the boy protested.

"You threw away your family's money."

"It was my money. And I donated it of my own free will."

"That's not what I heard."

"Meadlow, don't deceive the boy," I called out from the cot. "You admitted Tiagatha could do whatever he wanted with his inheritance."

The deprogrammer darted a look at me. "You're interrupting me again."

"The money was mine," the boy repeated.

"I don't deny that. What I'm disputing is whether you gave it freely. Your parents, they believe you were bilked out of it. You must have been tricked, embezzled. Maybe hypnotized into signing away your inheritance. Is that what happened? Don't be ashamed to admit it."

"Why, that's insane. I didn't sign away my inheritance. I donated part of it."

"How much?"

"I bought the communal tractor and some of the land, and I pay my share of the monthly bills."

"So what does that add up to?"

"It's none of your business. But I guess altogether I've contributed about twenty thousand dollars."

Meadlow threw back his head in a soundless guffaw. "And you wonder why your parents are worried."

"I thought they were worried about me, not my bank account."

"They're worried about your brain. You have to be cracked to waste that kind of money."

"You really think so? I've read about people—respectable businessmen like my father—who've contributed a lot more than that."

"Not to a bunch of crooks and charlatans."

"I wouldn't know. I don't call anybody those names. But hundreds of people donated more than twenty thousand to Nixon. Are you going to deprogram them? And how about the ones who gave to Wallace? Or are you part of his campaign team?"

Now it was my turn to toss back my head, and my guffaw was far from soundless.

"Very cute," Meadlow said. "We'll see how funny you and the Padre think it is after we've been here a few more hours. You better wise up, because I'm not joking."

"Neither am I. The money was mine, and I gave it willingly. But I suppose it's open season on anybody who makes an offering to a Pentecostal group."

"If it's not, it should be. What interests me, though, is what would make a man throw away that much bread."

"Faith," Tiagatha said. "A belief in what we're doing at the commune."

"That's what I'm getting at. What are you doing in that house? There must be some powerful attraction."

"There is. He's called Christ."

"You don't say? That still doesn't tell me what you do."

"We work in our garden. We pray. We read the Bible. We meditate. We try to be self-supporting and preserve our privacy. It's like a monastery," he said to me.

"How about fucking? You all get into any group gropes?"

"Watch your mouth," I said.

"I asked a question. What are these rumors I hear about sex orgies at the commune?"

"It's not true."

"You've got boys and girls together out there, and you're telling me they're not doing anything. What are they, queer?"

"Meadlow, you're making a fool of yourself."

"Let him answer."

Tiagatha sat on his hands to keep from shaking with rage. "We have a rule against sexual contact, except between bonded couples. The unbonded men and women sleep on separate floors."

"Bonded couples? You mean married?"

"Not as you understand it. They're couples who've taken a pledge in front of the rest of us to be faithful to one another."

"What you're saying is you've got unmarried couples living together. Do you realize this state has a law against lewd cohabitation? The police could slap you in jail for that alone. Now do you see why your parents are upset?"

"They weren't upset when I lived in a coed dorm at school. They didn't send anybody there to keep couples apart. It was only when I became a born-again Christian and moved in with other believers for holy company that they started hassling me. The minute I got my head straight, they clamped down on me. Did they tell you that?"

"Never mind what they told me." Meadlow looked restless, and as the boy evaded him, dancing beyond his grasp, it appeared to be causing the little man physical pain to maintain his patience. "Just once, why don't you try to see the situation from your parents' point of view?"

"I know their point of view. I lived with it more than twenty years. Now I have my own soul to save."

"Don't they have souls, too?"

"Yes. I tell them that all the time."

"But what are you doing to help them save their souls?"

"I pray for them. I beg them to repent. I . . . Why are you asking this? You don't believe in the soul."

"But you do. They do."

"I don't know what my father believes in besides money and television."

"Careful. You're presuming to judge again. And as for your mother, you know she believes."

The boy lowered his eyes.

Discovering a potential weak spot, Meadlow pressed harder. "I asked you before, do you love your parents?"

"I'm not going home," Tiagatha mumbled.

"Answer the questions in order. Don't you love your mother?"

Tiagatha nodded that he did.

"And your father?"

"Not after what he's done to me."

"Doesn't the Bible say to love everybody, even your enemies and sinners? Doesn't it tell you to turn the other cheek?"

"I don't have to let him wipe his feet on me. You're always yapping about logic. How does that make sense? You've met my father. Do you love him?"

"It's not my family."

I spoke up. "Did you love your own family?"

"Don't push me, Padre."

"The Bible says to love everybody," the boy repeated what Meadlow had said a moment before.

"I'm not a Christian. I don't *have* to love anybody."

"Is there anyone you love?" asked Tiagatha.

Meadlow looked trapped. "I don't believe in love. The term doesn't mean anything. It's just a misunderstanding of glandular activity."

"Then why are you asking if I love everybody?"

"Because you claim to be a Christian."

"All right," Tiagatha said, "I love my parents. Is that what you're after?"

"The Fourth Commandment orders you to honor them."

"Fine, I'll honor them. But I'm not going home. I love a lot of people, but I don't live with them, and I don't have to live *like* them. When the Bible says to love the sinner, it doesn't mean you should become one."

"Wait a goddamn minute. You're twisting my words. You've been so warped by religion, you're ignoring reality every time you open your mouth."

"Too bad for reality," the boy blurted. "In the beginning was the Word, not logic, not science, not your sort of rationality."

Meadlow acted as if Tiagatha had uttered an unimaginable obscenity. "See what you've done?" he asked me. "The kid's a mindless monster and you people made him that way."

"No, not him." Tiagatha refused to cut me in for a share of the blame or the glory. "Thaddeus taught me the truth. And now I'm free." He bounced to his feet.

"Don't bet on it, buddy. Sit down and shut up."

But before Meadlow had a chance to continue, Tiagatha was chanting and shaking in place. Almost instantly he was speaking in tongues, dancing in the spirit.

"Son of a bitch," Meadlow moaned, sinking onto his chair.

It was I who stood up and begged the boy to stop. "You're doing fine. Don't ruin what you've gained. Don't give Meadlow an excuse."

He skipped away from me, shimmying and yodeling, and in my frustration I had an urge to grab him and shake some sense into him. The fury I felt was that of a father toward a child who has humiliated him in public. Of a trainer toward a pet which won't perform.

My anger itself made me hesitate. I had no more right than Meadlow to demand that Tiagatha behave in a manner I approved. And it occurred to me this jitterbugging babble might be the boy's best protection. When under attack, he simply retreated into some obscure inner continent of self.

"Let's get out of here." Meadlow grabbed my elbow and led me into the blinding sunlight. "Satisfied?"

"What for?"

"For screwing me up. You're trampling all over my technique. Every time I get to an important question, you cut in.

I'd swear it was on purpose if I thought you were that smart. But it's just your bungling. From now on keep your trap shut when I'm talking."

"What's the matter, Meadlow, can't stand the competition?"

"You're not here to compete. You're supposed to provide a Catholic influence—whatever the hell that is! A fat priest muttering his beads, as far as I can see."

"You haven't seen me muttering any beads."

"Well, you ought to start that and stop interrupting me."

"You're blaming me, but it's the boy who's got your goat."

"Yes, he has, by acting like a damn moron. At your encouragement, I might add."

"Be honest. A lot of what he said made sense."

Meadlow jerked a hand toward the room. "You call that sense?"

"Did it ever dawn on you he might be doing it on purpose?"

"Of course he is. One minute he sounds like St. Thomas Aquinas, the next he's jabbering like an idiot. He's trying to knock us off balance. Divide us and duck between us."

"You can't blame him for protecting himself, and you'll have to admit he's doing a good job."

"My god! You've gone over to his side."

"I'm not choosing sides. But you're not going to change the boy. He's no fool. He has the brains to defend himself, and to slip away from you when he has to."

"You don't know what you're talking about. I've done dozens of tougher deprogrammings. The kid can't win."

"But he could keep us here forever."

"I've got forever," Meadlow said. "I'll stay as long as it takes. But I'm not about to stand in this heat scrambling my brains. If you have more on your mind, spill it at lunch." He took half a dozen brisk strides toward the cafe before glancing back over his shoulder. "Are you coming?"

"No."

"Good! Don't! You need to go on a diet."

I hurried to my room, intending to telephone someone and say this situation had to stop. Though I didn't entirely agree with Tiagatha, the boy's beliefs sounded no more absurd or dangerous than those of many people I met, and however much he may have annoyed his parents he didn't deserve this aggravation. Since I knew I couldn't convince the Hoovers to help or the police to step in, I decided to call Fr. Ryan.

But then, reaching the room, I didn't find a telephone and feared the only one at the motel might be in the U-Et-Yet Cafe. I was unwilling to risk using it with Meadlow nearby. If he overheard me, he might toss Tiagatha into the Chevy and speed off to a new place without me. I'd wait until he finished lunch.

Sitting down, I thought about the boy and what I'd tell Fr. Ryan. Despite my impatience, this cooling-off period was probably to my advantage. I needed time to reflect and formulate a plan. I couldn't phone and state flatly that the deprogramming was illegal, cruel and philosophically corrupt. Larry Sparks had said essentially the same thing that night at dinner and hadn't convinced Fr. Ryan.

I'd have to think of something better—maybe describe Meadlow's technique, which was a cross between a Socratic dialogue and the third degree. With megatons of energy, an agile mind and long memory, he seemed to have a simple strategy—keep pressing ahead, raising the same issues, repeating the same questions, hoping to harass Tiagatha until he collapsed.

Still, Tiagatha had stood up to him. That had amazed me, and was, I believed, what would impress Fr. Ryan. Although on the surface the boy might appear to be a pathetic cartoon of incoherence, there was strength and substance underneath. I wasn't sure I'd seen all the way to the bottom—any more than I had with Meadlow, whose veneer of reason seemed to conceal frightening volts of rage and resentment—but I was positive I could convince the pastor that we had no business abusing Tiagatha.

And then I'd . . . And then I'd what? If Fr. Ryan took my word, he'd order me home to St. Austin's. *Home?*

I sensed I was sawing a limb out from under myself. And out from under Tiagatha. It wasn't just that, wretched as it was here, I didn't care to return to the rectory. If I left, what would become of the boy?

Fr. Ryan could end my involvement, but that wouldn't stop Meadlow. Alone, the little man might do anything, and Tiagatha would have nobody to turn to. Not even someone to turn on when he needed to divert attention from himself.

Meadlow rapped on the door; I floundered to my feet. The deprogramming would have to go on, I guessed, until one of them dropped from exhaustion. Hungry and already fatigued, I wondered how long I could remain upright.

VI

Though no longer shivering and shaking and speaking in tongues, Tiagatha was still on his feet intoning a single prayer —"Lord have mercy on me, Lord have mercy on me, Lord have mercy on me"—and the coppery red of his beard and hair stood out around his face like an aureole of static electricity. He might not have sat down or quieted down since we left him an hour ago. Then again, he could have started this the instant he heard us at the door. I hoped so.

"Not this shit again," Meadlow said, in no mood to continue his calm, orchestrated approach. "I thought you gave up chanting."

Tiagatha didn't acknowledge the deprogrammer, although the little man had moved to within inches of him and, like a Marine Corps drill instructor, started shouting into his ear. Then Meadlow brought up his fists, and I thought he meant to slug the boy. But he clapped his hands instead, and Tiagatha's mouth snapped shut.

"I told you what the Bible says about vain repetitions."

"And I told you my prayers aren't vain, no matter how often I repeat them. Like a mantram, a prayer can gain significance the more you say it. It reduces the activity of the mind and liberates the soul for union with God."

"If the activity of your mind was reduced any more, we'd have to put you in a padded cell."

"Go ahead and insult me, but I've learned the secret of attaining peace that surpasses understanding."

"By spouting those Burma Shave slogans? Never happen. You're blinding yourself to the truth."

"No, I see much better now that I've been reborn. In the Bible it's written, 'It shall come to pass that your sons and daughters shall prophesy and your young men shall see visions.' "

"Is that what you were doing before lunch? I'm afraid I didn't understand heads or tails of that song and dance."

While they traded more insults and Biblical quotations, battling over every word, I resumed my uncomfortable roost on the cot. I could have used an infusion of that peace of which Tiagatha had spoken, for ever since I had recognized the abuse of his legal rights, I'd felt a growing pressure to grant the rightness of some of his beliefs, and I was reluctant to do that.

"Ask the priest if you don't believe me," Tiagatha said.

"What?" I mumbled. "I wasn't listening."

"Forget him. He's asleep at the wheel. You're a bright boy." Meadlow took a new tack. "A couple of times we've stood toe to toe slugging it out, and you gave as good as you got. But you can't go the distance with me, because you're fighting from weakness. Sure you can drag it out, but finally you'll fall with a thud."

"Are you going to let him turn this into a boxing match?" Tiagatha asked me. "What'll you do when the rough stuff starts?"

"There won't be any, and I don't agree with Meadlow. You're not fighting from weakness. You're capable of defending your faith."

"I shouldn't have to defend it."

"Do it anyway," Meadlow said. "The way things are these days, a lot of us have to learn to do what we don't like. You read the papers lately? The world's falling apart. Unless we find some solutions fast, we're doomed."

"Now *you're* talking like a prophet," Tiagatha taunted him.

"I'm talking like a man with good sense. We can't solve our problems until we face them squarely, and we won't face them squarely while our heads are cluttered with superstition and selfishness. That's all religion is—sheer selfishness. Because some fool is afraid he'll lose his nonexistent soul, he doesn't care a damn about helping his fellow human beings save their lives."

"A good Christian does both. He saves his soul *and* helps others. Sometimes he saves his soul *by* helping others."

"Personal charity! Church charity!" The little man burped on his lunch. "They don't change anything. For Chrissake, do yourself a favor and use your reason."

"You're like a broken record, Meadlow." Tiagatha raked a hand through his hair. "You keep talking about reason, but it isn't infallible. It can lead you wrong, too."

"Never."

"Yes, it can and it does."

"Impossible!"

"I see you haven't read Pascal's discussion of the paradox that reason itself should persuade a man that his reason is imperfect. Reason is the last thing to depend on in a religious debate."

Meadlow tossed his head. "What the hell are you babbling about?"

"I'm talking about the way human beings think, the way our minds function. From what scientists have learned, Pascal was right. Reason works from the raw material provided by instinct and the senses. But our instinct and senses are unreliable. Sometimes they can't even distinguish what's real from what's not. So isn't it clear if our senses are unreliable our reason must be limited and unreliable, too?"

The subject sank into silence for a moment. Maybe it had sunk into Meadlow as well. As it penetrated my own thoughts, I leaned forward, waiting for clarification, my head buzzing with abstractions.

"Who said anything about the senses?" Meadlow demanded. "We were talking about the state of the world, and how reason can solve our problems. You're the one who brought up this bullshit about instinct."

"Yes, to prove to you that if the brain depends on the senses, and our senses are unreliable, our reason is, too. Stop pretending it's the answer to everything."

Meadlow took a long look at Tiagatha, and then at me, as though I had put the boy up to this. Nodding, he said, "Now I get the picture. Our minds are imperfect—at least yours is—so we might as well forget thinking, give up on problem-solving and start jabbering and jumping around the room."

"Gimme a break, Meadlow. That's not what I said. I'm just pointing out the obvious—religion is a different order of experience. It has its own logic, and it's nothing like a computer's."

"That's for damn sure," said Meadlow. "I'd love to hear you explain the logic of religion."

The boy appeared eager for the opportunity, yet wary at the same time. "I only know how it was for me, and for a few kids at the commune. For me, faith didn't come from what I read or learned at school. It's a gift that grows out of anguish at our incompleteness, a hunger for immortality and for God's grace. I know what I feel and what I need, and your kind of reasoning doesn't tell me anything more about it. Faith is visionary. It's foundation is rapture and living communion and—"

"I've heard enough. How about you, Padre? You buy any of this?"

The boy looked to me, and I longed to back him up. Sloughing off his protective coloration, he had come into a clearing, daring to be explicit, and I wanted to hold him there—to help myself as well as him. Otherwise, I feared he might return to chanting and speaking in tongues. Yet my soul seemed to have shrunk so that his largeness of faith couldn't fit into it. All I could manage was his mother's words: "I believe."

"Big deal! Who gives a damn what you believe? It stinks in here."

Meadlow went out the door, slamming it thunderously behind him, and alone with the boy I feared I was no better than those tourists in Rome who had watched with wry curiosity while I said Mass. Here I was witnessing his struggle, perhaps hoping that if his faith survived, mine might, too, yet unable to do anything to help him.

"I believe," I repeated. "I swear I agree with a lot of what you say. But you won't change Meadlow's mind. Pascal in person couldn't do it."

"I thought it was worth bringing up anyway. I was tired of him treating me like an idiot."

"I understand, but—"

"But that doesn't matter either, does it? Your belief, your understanding, they won't change anything."

"I'd like them to."

"Then, for God's sake, do something."

"What?"

After a glance at the door, he moved from his chair to the cot beside me. "Let me go."

"Look, Tiagatha, even if I could manage it—and I can't—that wouldn't do any good. He'd catch you."

"Then I'd escape again. With your help, I could keep running until he got tired of chasing me."

"No, it wouldn't work."

"What you mean is, you won't help."

"It's not that." I leaned closer and whispered, "You don't

need my help, Tiagatha. You're doing fine. When you sit still and act sensible and answer his questions, you make a very good case for yourself."

Shaking his head, the boy smiled sourly.

"No, listen." I laid a hand on his shoulder. "I think he'll soon see how well you're holding your own and give up."

Still shaking his head, Tiagatha raised the cupped palm of his hand. "He's got you right there. Talking all the time about rationality, he has you thinking he *is* rational. He has you convinced I have to put up with his bullying."

"No, it's wrong for him to bully you. But you're frustrating him, defeating him, every time you offer a rational answer."

"Don't you see"—he strained against my hand—"the question isn't whether I can defend my faith rationally? I shouldn't have to. The minute you debate with him, you're playing his game, you're as much as admitting his questions are legitimate."

"Some of them are. You must have asked yourself many of the same questions."

"The difference is I asked *myself* and answered to *myself*. I don't have to satisfy his doubts. I only have to deal with my own."

"Okay." I signaled for him to hold his voice down. "Ideally, I agree with you. But this isn't an ideal situation. If you don't give that man straight answers, you're going to stay here."

"Unless you help me, Father, he's going to hold me here no matter what. And once he sees talking won't work, he'll knock me around the room."

"I'd never permit that."

"How could you stop it? If you're afraid to set me loose now, what could you do then?"

"If anything happens, I'll call your parents."

"They won't help."

"It won't go that far. It doesn't have to. You can call a halt to everything right now. You could go home and speak to your parents—you know, calmly and quietly—and change their minds. I'll go with you and make Meadlow wait outside in the car."

"No, no." He whipped his head from side to side. "You don't know them. I've tried talking. It doesn't matter how I say it, they'd still think I was crazy."

"But if you shaved and wore a suit and tie and didn't insist they call you Tiagatha, maybe they—"

He pulled back from my hand. "Has it helped you to take off your Roman collar and wear a sport shirt and tell people to call you Tony?" That blow must have done real damage to my face. Immediately, he said, "I'm sorry. You just don't understand. It wouldn't make any difference what I said to my parents, or how I dressed. It's not so much my name and beard and living at the commune they object to. It's what I've become. Now that I'm a believing Christian, they can't stand me. Please, Father, let me go."

With difficulty, I stood up. My knees crackled like dry twigs. "There's no way to do that, Tiagatha." Then, careful not to look back for fear he'd call out to me, I left.

I sat under the awning in a chair I had carried from my room and watched the sun sink beyond the horizon. The dust settled, the temperature plunged a precious few degrees, and the doves and swallows fled while the bats flickered through the gathering darkness. A breeze strummed the sagebrush and ocotillo spines, bringing meager relief from the heat but raising gooseflesh on my arms.

In the next shack Meadlow and Tiagatha were talking, arguing, skirmishing, their voices antiphonal and monotonous. The little man had hurried back in after I abandoned the boy, and I should have returned, too, but didn't believe there was any point, even though I recognized now what a deprogramming really was—an exorcism in which God, not Satan, was cast out.

The voices flared again. Meadlow was angry at Tiagatha, and the boy at him, and both of them at me. And if I phoned his parents or the priests at St. Austin's, they'd undoubtedly be angry at me, too. I was angry at myself. But what could I do? I was faced with leaving and having no influence. Or staying and not having much more.

"Hey," Zack hailed me from shack number one, "come on over and be sociable."

"Got plenty of beer," Billie promised, still in her blue robe, still sprawled massively with the armadillo on her lap. "Football game's on the tee-vee."

To avoid more fretting about the boy and my predicament, I picked up my chair and joined them. The Horskuses had a Sony portable television the size of a shoe box, resting on a table in front of them. I sat beside Billie and gladly accepted a can of Pearl, while Zack perched behind us, insisting, "I can see real fine." As he watched the screen between our shoulders, he had one hand on Billie's broad back, the other on mine. "I'm the quarterback here. Little Eddie LeBaron. And you two guys are the whole goddamn line." He gave us a rough, good-natured shaking, and we all laughed.

The Houston Oilers were at Oakland, and already the Raiders led by twenty points. As Billie analyzed it, "Their niggers are plain better than ours. Oops, sorry about that," she murmured to me.

"What the shit," Zack said, "ain't everybody from New York is a nigger. Tony looks like that on account of he's Italian."

"But you shouldn't use those words around a reverend."

"You mind?" Zack asked me.

"Well, I don't like the word 'nigger.' I've never cared for 'wop' or 'guinea' or 'hebe' or any racial epithets."

"I suppose you're right about them epaulets," Zack said. "Actually I admire hell out of the Nee-grows. When I was a boy and one of them pissed you off, you'd pop him in the mouth—their lips split real easy—and he'd run off and hide. But they've made miles of progress since then. Something's turned them tougher than a cob. Look at that number ninety-one. Ain't he a bad-looking mother? Why, I bet he could even beat up on old Billie here."

"Don't you count on it, son." She brandished a huge hairy fist. "I'd rap him upside his head so hard he'd ring like a church bell."

Cackling, Zack whacked her shoulder. "I believe it. I seen you do it before."

"Hell, you *felt* me do it before."

"That, too." His chuckle became shaky. "What we oughta do is arrange a rassling match between you and the Reverend. How about it, Tony?"

"Not me. I'm not at my fighting weight. Tomorrow morning I might start training with Meadlow."

"Maybe Meadlow's your man, Billie. He's little, but hard as a hickory nut."

"I'd bust him like a peanut."

Again we laughed, and when I belched on the beer we laughed louder. It felt awfully good. I couldn't remember the last time I'd had fun. But then Billie asked, "You really a priest?" and most of my enjoyment oozed away.

"Yes, I am."

"If that don't beat all. I never met one before. 'Course, I might have come close when I was with the carnival. We had all types out to see the show."

"That's for damn sure," Zack said. He seemed saddened by the memory.

"What sort of show was it?" I asked, to kill the discussion of my vocation.

"Aw, you know, just a dinky traveling carnival."

"Don't go running it down," Zack said. "We had stuck with it, we'd be retired to California by now, rich enough to fart through silk for the rest of our life."

"What happened?" I asked.

Billie turned on her tiny husband. "What do you say we drop it? Tony ain't interested in our troubles."

"Sure I am. Did something go wrong? When was this?"

"Well," Zack said, "asking me exactly what happened, exactly when I seen things going wrong, that's like asking a man backed his fanny into a buzz saw what tooth cut him first."

I laughed, but Billie shot Zack another intimidating look. "You're making a mystery out of nothing. I was the fat lady in that carnival," she told me, "when I all of a sudden started losing weight. Don't ask me why. I just lost interest in eating and couldn't hold any bulk on me. Sure, I'm still pretty damn big, but you gotta have something extra going for you if you aim to travel on the circuit. Because there's a very thin line between being a special attraction and plain being a slob. When I saw the changing looks on those customers' faces, I said forget it and retired."

"You didn't have to get hotheaded and quit the carnival. They gave you a choice," Zack said.

"Some choice," she snorted. "They swore to keep me on if I'd become a tattoo lady. What the hell kind of choice is that? I never had any fondness for needles, and I figure there are enough billboards around without me turning into one."

"I'd've done it in a minute. I told them that."

Now Billie burst into laughter. "Little as you are, Zack, it'd take both your ass cheeks to print a single rosebud on. But like I was saying, Tony, I never met a priest before."

"It's not so bad, is it?"

"No, indeed. You're a good old boy. But I feel like that I

ought to explain I don't go to church any more."

"Maybe you'll start again."

"Could be, but not unless we leave this place. I ain't about to drive down to Laredo every Sunday. Not that I've stopped believing in God. I suspect there must be one. I been all over this country with the carnival and seen just about every other weird thing you could think of, so it wouldn't surprise me none if there's a God. But let me tell you, Tony, if He is up there, He has one hell of a peculiar sense of humor."

"How's that?"

"Well, letting me lose weight ain't my idea of a knee-slapping joke, and leaving us here in this piss-ant place . . ."

Her voice trailed off as a pickup truck swung past the cafe and sped to the adobe shacks opposite us. In its high beams I saw the girls from the restaurant sitting outside their rooms, enjoying the evening air and drinking beer. They all wore loud miniskirts and loose-fitting blouses, except for one woman who was wrapped in a floral kimono and had her hair up in a rat's nest of curlers and papers.

When the truck lights winked off and the engine died, Billie said, "Son of a bitch. Is that Darlene in dry dock again?"

"Looks like it," Zack said.

"That woman ain't worth a lick of work. She was out all last week, blaming it on she was sick with sinuses. What's wrong with her this time?"

"She told me her head was still plugged up. I was you, I'd take her key and toss her out."

"And who are you going to get in her stead? She knows she's got us by the short hairs. But you march on over there and warn her to straighten out."

"Shouldn't I wait till those fellers leave?"

"No, do it now. Tell her next time she'll have me to answer to and I'll come out smoking."

As Zack trudged across the lot, Billie jiggled her knees up

and down, rolling the little armadillo around in her lap like a gleaming ball of mercury. "You know, Tony, it's a damn shame, but what folks say is true. You can't find dependable help no more."

The door to room six drew open, a rectangle of orange light slanted across the parking lot and Meadlow stepped out, casting an elongated shadow. As he approached us, there was a slope to his shoulders, a weary looseness at his joints, and I realized with relief that the boy hadn't broken.

"Want a beer?" Billie asked him.

"No, thanks." His voice was frayed.

"You look beat. Pull up a chair and watch the game."

"I'm not beat." He stiffened. "And I don't go for games."

"You don't like football?" she asked, incredulous.

"I don't like to watch or play *any* games."

"You must've been a barrel of fun at recess."

"Have you eaten?" he asked me. "Let's go to dinner. I've got something to tell you."

"Care to join us?" I asked Billie.

"Naw, I'll stick to Pearl." She was staring off to where Zack was scolding the woman.

The deprogrammer glanced in that direction. "Business appears to have picked up. I've never seen it this crowded."

"Yeah. Must be word-of-mouth advertising." Billie was bending her beer can. "You all better shake a leg. They'll be closing the cafe soon."

I stood up, thanked her for the beer and accompanied Meadlow to the cafe, which was quiet, bright and all but empty. While Cindy, the woman whose hair had been sculpted into a silver helmet, hung listlessly over the cash register like a dishrag spread out to dry, the Mexican boy, Chiquita Banana, shoved a broom up and down the sawdusted aisles. Meadlow and I slid into a booth where somebody had spent a long time blistering the table top with a lighted cigarette. As the boy swept by us, I lowered my gaze to the Formica and noticed that if I connected the burned spots they would add up to an armadillo.

"What's with that kid?" Meadlow asked. "He's staring at you like he knows you."

"He doesn't. How could he?"

"Are you sure you haven't been giving him a sermon or religious instructions?"

"I don't speak Spanish. He hasn't learned English."

"Maybe he suspects you're a Mexican, trying to pass."

"There are worse things to be."

"For Chrissake, don't get edgy."

"Who's edgy?" I asked, but the Mexican's deep, starved eyes did unsettle me.

Meadlow also seemed agitated. Although he had his hands in his lap, where I couldn't see them, I would have wagered he was squeezing, pushing and pulling. The stringy muscles of his neck had knotted. "You know, this arrangement we have really isn't working. We're already way behind schedule. I've been thinking you should stay out of the room while I'm talking to Tiagatha."

"No, that's why I'm here. To stay with him and provide a Catholic influence." I had repeated the phrase so often, it sounded foolish even to me.

"You think you're doing him any good?"

"That's not for me to judge."

"Then I'll judge for you. You're fouling things up, dragging them out, making it harder on him."

"I promised his parents and my pastor that I—"

"Okay, okay! Act as a Catholic influence, but do it on your own time. What I'm saying is, we ought to work in shifts—four hours on, four hours off. After I take a crack at him, you'll have your turn. I won't bother you, you won't bug me. How about it?"

Actually, I preferred this, for I detested being harassed by

Meadlow in front of the boy, and hated even more being humiliated by the boy in front of Meadlow. Still, I hesitated. "Aren't you afraid I'll spend my shift contradicting everything you tell him?"

"You're a panic, Padre. A regular laugh-riot. Be my guest. Contradict all you want."

"Don't worry. I will." With my finger I was tracing the dotted armadillo. "Are you married?"

He shook his head.

"Ever been?"

"No, and I won't ever be. I don't have the time."

"Time?" I asked. "Does it take that much?"

"Hell, yes, and a lot of money, and even more compromises and lies. I can live without that. I get enough sex to satisfy me. How about you?"

"I've never been married, either."

"That's not what I asked."

"I know."

"Well, how about it?" he insisted. "What's your position on sex?"

"I think the official Church position for priests is upright and an arm's length away."

"Aren't you interested in women?"

"Oh, I'm interested, all right. I *am* human, you know. But they're not likely to change the celibacy rule in my lifetime."

"Why wait? No one else seems to bother."

I quit fooling with the burned spots. "I don't know any women, anyway."

"You might meet a few if you slimmed down and bought some decent clothes and maybe let your hair grow a little. It looks like the busy end of a brush."

"You're not exactly a fashion plate yourself."

"I'm not the one looking to get married." He leaned forward. "But lemme get something straight. Are you saying you've never had a woman in your whole life?"

"That's right." I was aware of speaking defiantly. "I went into the seminary as a sophomore in high school."

"You may be the only virgin in America."

Sorry I had brought the subject up, I had nowhere to look except down at the armadillo again.

Meadlow surprised me by saying, "Hey, don't take it so hard. Believe me, you're not missing much. Most women are a dirty mess. Then they run to fat. And talk about emotional! Hang around one who's having her monthlies and she'll make Tiagatha sound like Bertrand Russell."

"I don't know anything about that. But lately the idea of being married and having a family—not that I have anybody in mind—sounds awfully appealing. But I guess it's too late for both of us."

"Speak for yourself. You may have varicose veins of the balls. I don't." Scooting around in the booth, he called to Cindy at the cash register. "Hey, are you awake?"

"Barely." She straightened herself on the strength of her fleshy arms.

"Where's the menu?" he asked.

"How many times do you have to see it? It doesn't change."

"What's today's special?"

"Calf and crawdad."

"What?"

"You know, your basic surf-and-turf special." She said it so it sounded like 'spatial.' "Chicken-fried steak and shrimp fried in batter and bread crumbs."

"Ugh! Gimme a hamburger, well-done, a salad without dressing and a quart of club soda."

"Couldn't interest you in cold cuts, could I? It's awful hot over that grill."

"I wouldn't eat anything here that hadn't been cooked to

a cinder. You'd die of trichinosis before you finished dessert."

"A good dose of it might clean your pipes."

Meadlow wasn't amused. "What'll you have?" he asked me.

"Same as this morning," I said to her. "A plate of sausages, hot cakes and syrup."

She shoved herself away from the cash register and strolled behind the grill. Though the floor was spotless by now, Chiquita Banana—what was his real name?—continued pushing the broom, and as he retraced his steps up our aisle I noticed he had greasy palm prints on his back as well as his chest. Had other people wiped their hands on his uniform?

"Why do you eat that crap?" Meadlow asked.

"It tastes good and it fills you up."

"Yeah, if you like sugar-coated glue. You realize what it does to your insides? Plugs up your bowels, puts pressure on your sphincter and causes hemorrhoids."

"Please, we're about to eat."

"Just telling the truth. You ought to watch your weight. Are you going to work out with me tomorrow morning?"

"Maybe. Wake me and I'll see how I feel."

"It'll do wonders for you. Look." He leaned back in the booth, yanked up his shirttail and smacked his bare flat belly.

"Yeah, terrific."

"Feel how solid."

"I'll take your word for it."

"No, come on. Punch it." He bounded up and around to my side. "Really let it have a shot. I won't feel a thing."

Cindy was watching us from under her helmet of hair. The Mexican boy had paused to watch, too.

To get it over with, I tapped Meadlow's stomach and nodded. "Nice and firm. Like a rock."

"You barely touched it." He belted himself several times. "See that? Didn't hurt me a bit. I do two hundred sit-ups a day." He returned to his side of the booth. "You should, too. A body's only as strong as its weakest muscle."

"That's one way of putting it."

"I'm serious. There's no sense letting your physique go to pot. I'm on a training program that leaves me mentally and physically fit for my work, and just as important, you see, I've willed my body to science. To the U.S.C. Medical School. I want to make sure they get something worth having. I figure my muscles and bones and brain should be in superb condition. So should my internal organs, if I eat right."

"That's a very noble and generous gesture, giving away your body."

"Not at all. It just makes sense not to waste perfectly good vital material. Someday we'll do it systematically, and once we learn how to utilize human vegetables—"

"Beg your pardon?"

"Human vegetables, people in comas. Before long, we'll use them as organ banks. By grafting spare parts onto dormant bodies, we'll be able to preserve organs and limbs until we need them. Of course, this'll require a lot more research into the cloning process."

As the deprogrammer went on to discuss what "we" would and wouldn't do once "we" had more data, I realized that if science was what he had instead of God this stockpiling of parts à la Frankenstein was his substitute for eternity. Though the soul, in his opinion, didn't exist, the muscles, bones and organs could be immortal.

"You know," he said, and there was rare emotion in his voice, "I wouldn't mind dying so much if I had lived to see that day."

I put out my hand to cover his and said as he had to me a

few minutes earlier, "I don't think you're missing much."

"Well, ain't that cute." Cindy plunked down our dinner plates. "A minute ago, you two fellers were fighting. Now you're holding hands."

Roughly, Meadlow brushed my hand aside.

VII

Sunday, shortly after dawn, I was down on my knees begging for mercy. Seldom have I prayed so fervently to be saved. After cajoling me to join him in simulated Marine Corps training, Meadlow had set a lung-singeing pace and a mile from the motel had run me to the ground, where I nearly impaled myself on a century plant. He'd circled back, then stood over me, jogging in place, while I heaved up my guts. "If you can't keep the pace, better wait right there. I'm going to do three or four more miles. See you on the return trip."

As he dashed on through the desert, disappearing into a heat mirage, I vomited twice more and still hadn't caught my breath when the dry heaves commenced. I would have been ashamed of my feebleness if I hadn't felt so sick, and I would have felt sicker yet if I hadn't been so frightened. Wondering whether Meadlow meant to abandon me here in the killing heat, I crawled around on all fours, frantically seeking protection from the sun. But these desert plants and bushes offered less shade than the skeleton of an umbrella.

Stretched out next to a spidery ocotillo with my ear pressed to the warm earth, I thought I heard hoofs. I lifted my head and spotted what looked like a tropical insect bobbing above the mesquite and chaparral. It was the deprogrammer, dressed in his sleek orange jumpsuit, jogging past scrub plants and prickly pear cactus, his shoes kicking up puffs of red dust.

"Fall in," he commanded, drawing on deep reserves of wind. "Off and on. Off your ass and on your feet. Work out those kinks. It doesn't help if it doesn't hurt."

I floundered upright, and that hurt plenty. Laboring after him, I wheezed and whined. My lungs burned, as did my feet, but I wouldn't let myself fall too far behind, for I dreaded being abandoned again.

The gnarled trees we trotted through grew no taller than my shoulders, and at first I felt like an ungainly giant in a forest, then as though my head had floated off on the string of my neck, dragging my body behind. As I lunged forward, the ground rose beneath my flared nostrils, filling them with dust and the odor of creosote tinged with vomit. A roll of flesh had flopped over my belt to swing like a pink half-cooked ham in the soaking net of my undershirt.

Near the motel, Meadlow widened the distance between us. The last thing he wanted was to be linked to this fool who was blue in the face, his belly bouncing out of control. On the parking lot he sprinted a final few laps before I arrived to a chorus of catcalls and Bronx cheers from Billie, Zack and the girls. I stumbled to my room, turned on the shower and fell into a fetal position on the tile floor.

Outside, Zack had finished flicking slugs onto the asphalt and cackling as they evaporated. Then, like an insane auctioneer or hog caller, he completed his instructions to Chiquita Banana, and I could picture him churning his arms and winking behind the boy's back at Billie.

I sat in my room, shivering beside an air-conditioning vent, and told myself I should say Mass. I had brought my travel kit with me, and on the combination chest of drawers–desk–and–

vanity table I could have arranged an altar. Yet I couldn't bear to confront the mirror, murmuring the words to my own face and to the reflection of the spavined bed, the cinder block walls, the gooseneck lamps.

The way I felt, it wouldn't have mattered if I'd had a full congregation and the Vatican choir. With blisters the size of silver dollars on the balls of my feet, I couldn't stand for more than a few minutes. My arms and legs twitched while I was motionless and tormented me with cramps when I moved, and every breath brought the foul taste of bile to my mouth.

I assured myself I was justified in taking sick leave. Yet down in the darkest, dankest corner of my soul, I realized that sick or well at home or in transit, I wouldn't have cared to say Mass this Sunday. My physical collapse seemed to have precipitated another spiritual decline. Could a mental one be far behind?

Someone knocked at the door, and assuming it was Meadlow I sullenly said, "Come in."

There was another knock.

"I told you, come in."

Chiquita Banana, blinking timidly, craned his neck around the door, then stepped in dragging a broom. Although he wore the same once-white uniform, he smelled of sweet floral soap and hair oil, and eyed me with an almost animal inquisitiveness. To escape the disturbing depths of his gaze, I concentrated on the blank TV screen until suddenly he swept in front of me. The broom clattered to the tile, and he dropped to his knees, kissed my hand and murmured, *"Perdóneme, Padre, porque he pecado. Hace tres meses que no me confieso."*

I didn't need to speak Spanish; there was no mistaking his meaning. When I drew back my hand, he groped for it, eager for the physical contact.

"Perdóneme, Padre . . ."

"Who told you? How did you know?"

He flinched at my gruffness. *"He pecado."*

"I can't help you. Don't you see, I'm not a—" I stopped short of denying I was a priest. "I'm not from this parish. You'll have to go to Laredo. Go to *Laredo.*" I gave the city what I thought was the Spanish pronunciation.

"Hace tres meses que no me confieso." The boy was bewildered.

"Non parlo spagnuolo." I pitched to my feet.

"Que dice?"

"It's impossible." I flailed my arms to signal enough, finished. *"Impossibile.* This isn't my parish," I repeated.

But more than anything, I didn't want to listen to words that I didn't understand, then respond with ones that the boy wouldn't comprehend. I couldn't conceive how it would help to pass his contrition through the cracked alembic of my soul.

"Por favor, Padre, ayúdeme."

As I backed toward the door, he pursued me on his knees, crawling across the tile. I had seen people perform such penances in Italy, mortifying the flesh, shaming me with the strength of their faith.

"Get up. Please stand up." I started to hoist him by the elbows, but stopped short, afraid my hands might leave black prints. "You don't need me."

"No entiendo," he said.

"Non capisco," I said.

After a few desperate gestures, I left. Meadlow sat in front of his room reading and I rushed at him.

"Did you tell the Mexican boy I'm a priest?"

He finished a paragraph before folding the book—the Bible—on his finger. "What's with you?"

"That boy, did you tell him I'm a priest?"

"I haven't said a word to him. Billie or Zack must have told him."

"No, he doesn't understand English."

"Do they?"

"Very funny. They don't speak Spanish, and he doesn't speak English. So how does he know?"

"He obviously understands more than he admits. Or maybe he saw your priest clothes or something. Are you ashamed that he knows the truth?"

"Don't be silly. It's just strange, that's all. But I suppose you're right. He saw my travel kit."

"Your what?"

"The kit I use to carry the equipment for administering the sacraments." I pressed a hand to my moist forehead. "I still don't feel right after this morning. Tomorrow I'm going to set my own pace."

"Careful those slugs Zack fools with don't catch you."

"You're in a jolly mood. What happened, you find a juicy passage in the Bible?"

Meadlow held it aloft, looking at it back and front. "It's the same from cover to cover. A crock of shit. But the boy's depending on it again. The way he talked this morning, he must have stayed up all night memorizing obscure verses."

"Stumped you, did he?"

"Don't get your hopes up. He can run, but he can't hide."

"I'll take my turn now. Let me have the key."

Ignoring my outstretched hand, Meadlow laid aside the Bible, went to the next room and unlocked the metal flange. When I stepped inside, pausing just beyond the threshold as my eyes adjusted to the change from sunlight to lamplight, he shut the door and locked it.

"Hey, what are you doing? Unlock that door."

"Can't do it, Padre. I wouldn't want you to get any ideas about freeing our friend."

"What if there's an emergency—a fire or something?"

"Holler. I'll be nearby."

"I'm locked up in here all the time," Tiagatha said. "Didn't you ever think of that?"

"He's right outside," I said, attempting to compose myself before facing him. "There's no real danger."

Tiagatha shut his miniature Bible and shoved it into the holster on his belt. Though paler after a few days indoors, he looked alert and healthier than I felt, and his clothes were clean, if a bit wrinkled. He must have washed them each evening and hung them to dry overnight next to the air conditioner. He might have dried himself there, too. His hair and beard were wilder and more windblown than yesterday.

I carried a chair over near the cot, so as not to sit eyeball to eyeball with the boy. We both stared at the far wall, as if waiting for a slide show.

"By the way, do you speak Spanish?"

"No."

"You swear? Not a word?"

"No. What are you getting at?" He was tense, anticipating a new line of attack.

"Have you talked to the Mexican boy who cleans the rooms?"

"What Mexican boy? Nobody's been in here but Meadlow and you."

As he folded his arms, I crossed my aching legs. Troubled as I was about Chiquita Banana, I might have derived some pleasure from the thought that he had recognized me as a priest if there weren't a worm within that tiny kernel of potential pride. I felt I was being pursued, hounded. First the doorman, then Lenny and Rita, and now Chiquita Banana.

"What is this?" Tiagatha asked. "The silent treatment? Aren't we going to argue about religion and the right way to save my soul?"

"Not unless you'd like to."

"Don't tell me it matters what I want."

"Of course it does." I tried to calm the boy, who had become irritable and aggressive, realizing he could get away with it when Meadlow wasn't around. "We'll talk about whatever you like."

"That's big of you. For a priest, you're not very good at preaching, are you?"

"Meadlow thinks I do too much of it. But you're right, I'd rather answer questions."

"You're working overtime to prove you're my buddy. But why dump on Meadlow? You're no better than he is. You're certainly not as smart."

I concentrated on the wall so he wouldn't see the blood rush to my cheeks. "Yes, much as I disagree with him, he's a remarkable man in some ways. Too bad he isn't on our side."

"Our side! Will you quit playing Mr. Nice Guy? Of course you don't agree with Meadlow. But you're using him. You're setting it up so you'll look good by comparison." He got to his feet and circled me. "I've known from the start what you're up to. You think if you sit tight I'll wear myself out arguing with Meadlow, then you can drag me back to the Catholic Church."

"I'm not dragging you anywhere. Today I hardly have the energy to drag myself around."

"You mean to say you don't want me back in the Church?"

"Not if you don't believe in it."

"Well, I don't. So what are you after?"

"I'm not after anything, except maybe to convince you I care about your well-being, regardless of what religion you follow."

"With everybody caring about me so much, why was I kidnapped, why am I being held here with Meadlow hollering at me all day?"

Now that he was shouting at me, I understood how bad it was for him. "I don't have any control over that."

"That's a cop-out. What can you control? What good are you?" This time he saw my face and said, "Forget it. Don't take it so hard. Meadlow's methods must be rubbing off on me." He flopped onto the chair. "You begin fighting him and pretty soon you become as bad as him." He shook his head. "Know what he said this morning? He told me my kind of religion was like committing suicide without dying—a living death. He must have gotten that from my parents. They're always telling me what a waste it is, how unhappy I must be. But I have a lot of friends and we were enjoying ourselves in the hills. What's wrong with that?"

I knew of nothing wrong with it, and he drew encouragement from my silence.

"I'll tell you what *is* wrong. Most people are afraid to act on their faith, afraid they'll offend somebody. But as soon as that happens, religion is reduced to an empty ritual or a second-rate organization for social work."

"Don't be so quick to knock that. There's a lot of work to be done, and churches overlooked it for too long."

"Okay, but is that the whole answer? Even after you've filled everybody's belly and built roofs over their heads, they'll still feel incomplete. And that's where God comes in—where everything else ends."

A headache had begun to tighten around my skull, and I struggled to regain my grip on the conversation and guide it toward other areas. "You said you have friends at the commune and enjoy that life. Tell me about it."

"What do you mean?"

"What's it like out there? Who are your friends? Do you have a girl?"

"Has Meadlow been spreading rumors about orgies again?"

"No, please trust me. We're running in circles. It makes me dizzy. If you'd rather not tell me, we'll keep quiet."

"Well, I don't want to talk about my girl, and there's not much to say about the commune except that it's peaceful and private."

"What do you do during the day? You mentioned you grew your own food."

"Yes, most of it. Then we truck the surplus and some of the crafts we make down to The Drag and barter for what we need. I guess it's not very efficient, but it's fun and it keeps us in touch with students at the University. We talk to them, and invite them out to the house from time to time."

"You talk to them about religion?"

"Yeah, that and other things. Sometimes we get new ideas, sometimes they do."

"Do you invite other people, older ones, out there?"

"Sure, they're welcome. My mother's been there a couple of times. But, you know, it turns a lot of them off. Just our names make some of them mad. When we see them getting uptight, we try to stay loose and sing a few songs or go swimming. We're right next to the lake."

"Sounds nice."

"Believe me, it is, especially compared to what I've been through the last few years."

"What's that?"

Tiagatha tugged at his beard. "This is beginning to sound too much like Twenty Questions. Or a counseling session."

"Sorry. I didn't mean to pry. I guess I've gotten used to this sort of one-sided conversation. Confessions, you know. And then, uh, I went through a bit of counseling myself recently."

"How's that? Did you flip out?"

There was nothing oblique about Tiagatha. "You might say so. They called it a breakdown, but I've always thought of it as a slowdown. I was upset and had to take it easy for a while and do some thinking about my vocation. They sent me to Rome to rest."

"How do you feel now?" The boy seemed earnest. He always did.

"Better in most ways. But I still have a few things to work out."

"I know what you mean. I never had a breakdown, but I went through some really bad scenes at college. My folks sent me to Yale. It's a good school, I guess, but . . ." He shrugged.

"It must have been a big change."

"Yeah, coming from here it was. You know, the weather and New England and urban living and everything. But the worst thing was just deciding who I am and what I want to be. When I first went away, I did it all by the numbers. I drank a lot, I took drugs whenever I could get them, I slept with any girl who'd let me. I was what they call 'normal.' Nobody bothered me. Nobody even noticed. My parents knew some of the things I did—I mean, I wasn't hiding—and they seemed to approve, like it was part of growing up and becoming an adult.

"But I was miserable the whole time. When I told them so, they said that was normal, too. But nothing made sense to me, and my life seemed headed nowhere. That's when a friend, a fellow in the dorm, started talking to me about Jesus. Of course, I'd gone to Catholic schools and I'd always heard about Him. But now He answered my questions and changed my life. Changed it in ways I never expected."

"How's that?"

"Maybe I was silly for thinking things would stay the same. I sure never expected I'd drop out and join a commune. I thought everybody would be happy for me because I felt better again. But they treated me like I was nuts and I saw how twisted our lives have become without God. I realized those guys at college and my parents were willing to let me do almost anything except commit myself to the Lord. They prided themselves on being tolerant toward every sort of strange behavior. It was only religion they wouldn't stand for. I knew then I had to put distance between them and me. But, of course, after accusing me of being crazy and brainwashed, my parents hired Meadlow to kidnap me and brainwash me back into being their obedient little boy. Have you ever heard anything to top that?"

"Yes. I think so. The story of St. Thomas Aquinas." I spoke

slowly, struggling against nausea. My headache had developed hazy side effects, and I had a hard time sitting up straight. "When he decided to become a priest, his parents were enraged. They were a wealthy family and didn't want to lose him to the clergy. They spent all their time trying to change his mind. Finally, when he wouldn't listen any longer, they got a prostitute to come into their home and locked her in a room with Thomas, thinking she'd seduce him back to the worldly life."

"What happened?"

"That I don't remember. But I assume he got out safely. After all, he is a saint."

"Hey, are you okay, Father? You look like you're turning green."

"It's my head. And my stomach. I've been sick since this morning."

"You better lie down."

"Later. I don't like to leave you with Meadlow any more than I have to."

"Here, use my bed." He urged me up and over to the cot. "Is something wrong with your legs, too? You're limping."

"It's my feet. The soles are burning."

"Let me take off your shoes."

"No, I'll do it."

But when I sat on the cot and bent over, my head spun and I slumped onto my side. He had to roll me to the center of the canvas, loosen my laces and pry off my shoes.

"My God! You're bleeding. There's blood all over your socks."

"The blisters must have popped."

He wasn't listening as he stripped away my damp socks. "Lord, what is this?" His voice had taken flight a few octaves, and I was afraid he would think I had the stigmata and start speaking in tongues.

"It's nothing," I said. "I went jogging with Meadlow. He's working me into shape. You'll have to admit I should lose a lot of weight."

"I'll wet a towel and wipe up the blood."

"Don't bother."

But he went into the bathroom and was running the water. Then he came back, and I sighed as the damp cloth cooled my stinging soles.

"You're a strange sort of priest," he said.

"These days, what other kind could I be?"

"I don't know. Most of them act so superior and condescending, especially around me. It's like they think they alone have the truth. What's the matter? Don't you believe any more?"

"No, I believe."

"If you haven't lost your faith, what's the problem?"

"I . . . I guess I've lost everything except my faith. I believe, but what good does it do?"

"No good at all unless you act."

"How? I always thought faith would change my life, let me see things clearly."

"Faith by itself won't change anything. You have to put it into practice."

"Sometimes I just don't see the purpose."

"The main purpose is to save your soul."

"Somehow my own soul doesn't seem very important."

"Don't say that." The boy squeezed my foot, and I yelped in pain. "Sorry. But you shouldn't say that. Your soul is the most important thing in the world."

Although I realized I would sound like Meadlow, I had to ask, "How can you be so sure?"

"I feel it."

"But how?"

"Would a man like Meadlow spend so much time trying to

stamp out faith if there was nothing to it? Would he work so hard at destroying souls if they didn't exist?"

"I don't know. I just don't know."

"I think you better make up your mind what you do know, Father." He was busy dabbing the cloth at my feet again. "You can't go on the way you are. It must be tearing you apart."

"It is. But what am I supposed to do—spend my life like some medieval monk preserving relics and antiques that nobody else cares about? My God, I feel like a museum keeper."

"That doesn't sound so bad to me. But if it helps you, why not look at yourself as someone whose vocation is to preserve the meaning of the museum, the belief that stands behind the building?"

"Is that enough? What about the rest of the world?"

"We can't change it unless we keep our own faith first."

Then Meadlow jabbed his key into the doorknob and Tiagatha tore away from me, back to his chair.

VIII

"My turn," Meadlow declared.

I struggled to my feet and headed for the door. Though I had more questions for Tiagatha, I didn't care to ask them in Meadlow's presence.

"Hey, wait a minute. Forget something?" He kicked at my shoes and socks. "What the hell is this?"

"My feet were bleeding. The blisters popped."

He sucked in his breath, and after I retrieved what belonged to me he followed me outside, whispering viciously, "What are you doing, sabotaging me? You take off your shoes during a deprogramming and you immediately lose your psychological advantage. That kid's jerking you around like you're on roller skates."

"My feet *were* bleeding." I shook the bloody socks in his face.

"So what? Soak them in salt water. Jeezus, you better toughen up or you're not going to last."

I hobbled toward my room. Early as it was, Billie and Zack had assumed their stations at the television set outside unit number one, and when Zack glanced up he waved and shouted a welcome. Waving in answer, I went into my room and, standing unsteadily over the toilet, stuck a finger down my throat and choked up a yellow string of bile. That brought very little relief.

Moving to the sink, I brushed my teeth to rid my mouth of the taste of vomit. Then, bending painfully at the waist, I shot a gob of watery toothpaste into the porcelain bowl and watched something awful crawl out of it. An insect scuttled around the sink, shaking off flecks of foam. A miniature lobster, it waved its claws and twitched its question mark of a tail.

I dropped the toothbrush, and my belly heaved at the sight of the scorpion, but nothing came up. Had that thing been inside me? Considering the state of my stomach, mind and soul, I could almost believe it.

Tempted to touch the barbed stinger, I thought that would end it. Or serve as a salutary jolt. The sharp puncture, the spreading poison, might bring into focus the unspecified pain I had been feeling for months. But before I could budge, the scorpion was slipping on the porcelain, sliding toward the drain. Its flicking tail dropped down the hole, then its claws, pinching air. I turned on the hot water to make sure it didn't crawl up again.

In the other room there wasn't one safe spot. If I sat on the bed, I saw myself in the mirror. If I sat in a chair, the television screen reflected my face. I couldn't bear the sight, and when I shut my eyes, my head spun. Pulling on dry socks and my shoes, I left, realizing I had to do something, try anything.

Zack whooped and waved once more, but I explained to Billie and him in passing that I hadn't had breakfast or lunch and needed a bite to eat. There were few people in the cafe, none of them near the telephone on the wall at the far end of the row of booths. I went to it and dialed a number indicated in red with flames licking at the letters, FOR EMERGENCIES.

"Help you?" asked the operator.

I turned my back to the sparse crowd. "I'd like to speak to the police," I whispered.

"Beg pardon."

"The police. Let me speak to the police."

After ten rings, an Officer Broyles answered.

"I have a kidnapping to report."

"Your name?" he asked, voice flat and uninflected.

"That doesn't matter."

"It does to us."

"I'd rather remain anonymous."

"Where you calling from?"

"That doesn't matter, either."

"Sir, this is standard procedure."

"This isn't a crank call. I witnessed a kidnapping. I know where the criminal has the boy. He's there now. You can catch him."

"Okay, where?"

"A motel near Encinal. It's off the highway a few hundred yards. A place called Billie and Zack's Adobe Shacks."

"Hey, who are you, anyway?"

"Forget that. There's a boy being held prisoner."

"What are you, one of his friends?"

"Yes."

"You mean you're a Jesus Freak, too?"

The phone felt slippery and alive in my palm. "Look, I'm trying to report a crime. Let me speak to your superior."

"I am my superior."

"Then you're shirking your duty."

"I was you, friend, I wouldn't go around telling folks their duty. I know what I'm doing. So does Noland Meadlow."

I carefully placed the receiver in its cradle and limped past the booths toward the door.

"Don't you want something to eat?" Cindy sang out from behind the cash register. "Try the tacos today."

I plunged into the heat of the parking lot and across it to Billie and Zack. There was nothing to do except join them. Better to watch that noisy box, I thought, than to contemplate my utter uselessness.

"Back already?" Billie asked. "You ain't had time for a snack, even."

"I've decided to go on a diet."

"That's a shame. I swear I ain't seen nothing like you this morning," Zack said. "At least not since the reform mayor chased Wanda Sanchez out of Nuevo Laredo. Remember her, Billie?"

"Sure. She was the one could spin her titties like airplane propellors. She'd have one headed this-away and the other that direction. That girl had a million bucks right there in her boobs if she'd stayed out of trouble."

"Here, take a load off." Zack shoved a chair toward me. "Got us a ball game going."

"Want a cold brew?" Billie asked.

I glanced at the sky. It was late afternoon, but I decided to call it early evening, hoping a beer would settle my stomach. "Thanks, I will."

"No football today," Billie said, as Zack zipped into their room. "Baseball instead."

"It doesn't matter."

"Me, I never did care for it. Not enough knocking in it. 'Course, you'll have your occasional head-bumping on the base lines, but that's hardly worth bothering about."

"It's a lot rougher than it looks, let me tell you," Zack said, passing me a can of Pearl. "Ever play, Tony?"

"Not much. In New York we played stickball. At the seminary, they discouraged baseball and warned us about injuring our canonicals." I pressed my index finger and thumb together.

"What'd I tell you?" he asked Billie. "They ain't wearing pads, you know. Somebody slams one of them high hoppers down the third-base line and smacks you in the canonicals and you'll wish to hell you never set foot on the field. Ain't that the truth though, Tony?"

I was forced to smile and nod.

"Yeah, I been hit in the canonicals a couple of times," Zack observed. "Hurts like a bitch, but I never missed my turn at bat."

"Oh, quit bragging on how tough you are. Where's Meadlow?" Billie asked me.

"In with the boy."

"He whomping that hippie yet?"

"No, he doesn't hit him. He talks to him."

She snorted, shaking a few layers of fat. "I wouldn't believe that if he was to swear on a stack of Bibles. I been around enough bastards like him to know the littler the man, the more he enjoys jumping on folks."

"I don't," Zack swore.

"Ain't talking about you. But I remember the time you cold-cocked that cowboy in Alice with a beer bottle."

"Yeah, I reckon I like to drove that booger right into the ground. They had to pry him up with a crowbar."

When their laughter subsided, I said, "I don't think Meadlow's like that. I don't agree with his ideas, but he's well-respected. The boy's parents tell me he's been on television."

"Who you kidding?" Billie eyed me askance. "If business was better, I wouldn't let him use those rooms."

"You don't have much choice, do you?" Zack said, zeroing in obsessively on his grievance. "Ain't nothing about to get better around here unless they condemn us."

"They won't, so why bitch about it?" She crushed an empty beer can in one hand as we stared off at the Interstate, where traffic streaked by as silently as eye floaters. "We're too damn far from the road."

"They might could widen it."

"To what, twenty-six lanes?"

"I don't see no sense in giving up. I had my way," he told me, "we'd burn the place to the ground and collect on the inn-surance."

"Zack, drag your head out of your ass. You want cops and firemen poking around here?"

"Well . . ."

"Well nothing. I'd a damn sight rather live here than rot in the slam."

He granted that he would, too, but insisted, "We oughtta go a different route, then. Expand the operation. Pretty up the place. Maybe put in a swimming pool and a Putt-Putt range."

"That'd be throwing bad money after good."

"No, Billie, I read this magazine claimed you gotta go big time if you aim to make it. There's motels in California that have steambaths and bowling alleys and pool tables and pinball machines. There ain't no room for the small businessman any more."

"I ain't no small businessman," her voice boomed. "So drop it."

Mustache twitching, Zack swung around to me and asked, "You ever been to California?"

"Never have."

"Me neither. But I always had an itch to visit them orange groves. They say you can reach up and grab as much as you want." He made a motion like a man milking a cow.

"You got it confused with Florida," said Billie. "I been to the Coast two, three times, and it's nothing but smog and freeways. Here, go pop me a Pearl." She lifted the baby armadillo onto her lap and tickled its soft underbelly till Zack was out of earshot. "I don't know what to do about him, Tony. He's sick with worrying over the business."

"I wish there was some way I could help."

"There ain't, and that's the problem. We're stuck in a spot where can't anybody help us, and ain't nobody ever going to bother condemning us. But Zack, he still has these ideas about breaking into the big time. You know, hooking up with a brand-name chain or buying in on a franchise. We're about as likely to do that as I am to sprout a third tit."

After Zack returned with the beer and we resumed our conversation, accompanied by the desultory sound effects of the baseball crowd, one of the girls emerged from her room and strolled across the parking lot. She wore a green rayon robe and a pair of green slippers with pompoms on the toes. Like the other girls, she had hair as gaudy as a neon sign, hers the color of a Bloody Mary. Flourishing what looked to be a pink four-battery flashlight, she announced in a petulant voice, "This won't work. I'm on duty tonight and it's dead. You got any extra batteries?"

"In on the chester drawers," Zack muttered with an elaborate display of disinterest. Billie, nursing a beer, ignored her.

The girl brushed past me and came back a moment later loading batteries into the extraordinary device which, I noticed, had neither a lens nor a bulb, and was round at one end. Finally I recognized the gadget, feeling foolish for not having known at once what it was.

"Ain't that some shit," Zack said as the girl fancy-strutted across the lot, the green slippers slapping at her heels, the pink wand poised in her hand like a drum majorette's baton.

"I thought you told them they had to pay their own expenses," Billie growled.

"I did. But Darlene don't care what you tell her."

"You let some women have an inch and they want a mile," Billie said.

"You let Darlene have about six inches and she'll sit up and smile," Zack corrected her.

But it was Billie who smiled. "Goddamn, you don't quit, do you? You keep piling up like rent. I swear, it wasn't for your sense of humor, Zack, you wouldn't be worth nothing."

She sprinkled beer on his hair while he sat there, head bowed, very proud of himself.

I, too, had my head bowed, and my face fixed in a perplexed expression. They didn't seem to notice. At any rate, they didn't act as if they owed me an explanation or so much as a comment concerning what was obvious. I suppose a better priest might have spoken up angrily and raised moral and legal objections. But what was the use? Having let so much pass, how could I start complaining now? I had never harangued the prostitutes who hustled me in New York City. I didn't preach to the people lined up for porno movies. Since I couldn't save them, couldn't offer anything except feeble encouragement, I felt I had no right to criticize. Like Billie and Zack, everybody appeared to be trapped in a tight spot where, although they might be condemned or saved eventually, they somehow had to survive day to day.

As evening advanced, the colors that had been bleached from the land slowly seeped back. A brilliant orange flared from behind the horizon, shading into purple and mother-of-pearl as it spread east. On the plains around the motel the skeletal bushes seemed to regrow greyish-green leaves, and a breeze swept through them, a dry, spicy breath from Mexico. While insects the shape and nearly the size of Havana cigars commenced their twilight sawing, Billie spread her arms, shaking back the sleeves of her robe and sighing. "Aaah, don't that feel good?"

Meadlow slammed the door to unit six and locked up, looking even more slope-shouldered and weary than I felt. When he saw us huddled around the TV set, he hesitated.

"Care for a cold brew?" Billie called.

"No." He strode toward us.

"We ain't got any of your bubble water here. But Zack'll fetch a bottle from the cafe."

"I'm not thirsty." He leaned against an awning post.

"Take my chair," Zack said.

"No, I've been on my ass for hours."

"Hell, we don't need to watch this," Billie said. "I know how you feel about games. We'll switch to another channel. What's your favorite show?"

"Don't bother. I'll just stand here and finish decompressing."

I could easily understand their solicitude. Anyone could who saw Meadlow slouch against that post, hands deep in his pockets, miserably small and pale. He looked like a lost child, and then a moment later, when the light changed, like a troubled old man. I almost expected Billie to gather him onto her lap along with the armadillo and mother him.

After a few minutes, Zack hopped up and went inside—to pop another Pearl, I assumed. But he brought back a big yellow balloon and sang "My Country 'Tis of Thee" in the high-pitched voice of a castrato. Shocked, I let a slug of warm beer slide down the wrong pipe.

When the air had rushed from Zack's lungs, his voice returned to normal. But he took a deep drag on the balloon and broke into a squeaking rendition of "Abide with Me." I started giggling and couldn't stop. Billie chuckled, too, though she didn't appear surprised.

"What is this?" I asked, fighting to catch my breath.

"Zack's had his balls cut off," Billie said.

"There's helium in the balloon," Meadlow explained matter-of-factly.

"Spoilsport," Zack squealed, and his voice cracked and dropped into character. "Here, you have a whiff."

Meadlow batted the balloon away from his face. "Find another guinea pig."

"I'll take a turn." Billie grabbed the balloon, which was still half-inflated, and inhaled all the air into the huge bellows of her lungs. Then sky-high on helium, she serenaded Meadlow with a tart sea chantey entitled "Careful Sailor Boy, or I'll Cut Off Your Seafood." The baby armadillo scrambled bolt-upright, sniffing at her left breast.

When Billie reached the refrain for the fourth time, Zack ducked into the room and brought out a dozen more inflated balloons, each attached by a string to his fist. One of them looked suspiciously like a reservoir-tipped prophylactic. He divided them among us, excluding Meadlow, then passed around Magic Markers.

"What's going on?"

"It's Sunday! Advertising night!" Billie said, her lungs empty at last.

Zack was scribbling "Billie & Zack's Adobe Shacks" and the address and phone number on the balloons he held. "It's a trick we learned working for the carnival. Best damn publicity in the world."

"It's the cheapest, anyway," Billie added.

"It can't be much better," Meadlow remarked, "than stuffing a message in a bottle and tossing it overboard."

"That's your opinion, smart-ass. Won't you never let nobody enjoy hisself?"

"You'd be surprised the results we get," Billie promised the deprogrammer.

"You mean those balloons have actually improved business?"

"Oh hell, yeah. We been busier than a couple of one-legged fellers in an ass-kicking contest. Go ahead, write down your address on a balloon and see don't your business get better."

"No, thanks."

"Why not? What do you have to lose?"

"It's stupid."

"A lot sillier things work every day. Unbend a bit, Meadlow. You're stiff as a man in cardboard underwear."

"How about you, Tony?" Zack asked.

"I don't have anything to advertise."

"Sure you do. God! Put your name on that big red one and say you're searching for lost souls."

I didn't care to confess that the one lost soul I was looking for was my own, and I had no idea what I could write on a balloon to recover that.

When he had finished inscribing all the balloons, Zack

stepped from under the awning and launched his bright bobbing advertisements. A breeze lifted them out over the plains, then a sharp downdraft sent them scuttling and snagged nearly half of them in the tangle of mesquite bushes.

"They're caught!" Meadlow shouted.

"Some of them are still sailing."

"They won't be for long."

Zack shrugged. "We'll send up another batch tomorrow evening."

"Why don't you go out and shake them free?"

"It's no big deal. They look pretty there in the bushes."

"Are they biodegradable?"

"Say what?"

"You're cluttering up the environment with your nonsense."

Zack glanced around. "Seems like somebody got a head start on me. But if you're so worried about it, go on out and take them down."

"I will, since you're obviously too lazy." Meadlow looked like Lenny that last night in New York—a razor blade that had been stropped too often. Tiagatha seemed to have worn him to a jagged edge, and now he was slashing away at anybody nearby.

"Suit yourself," Zack said. "But don't expect me to tweeze the stickers out of your ass."

As the little man sprinted into the fields, the three of us drew closer to the TV as if for warmth. Soon the first cars and pickup trucks cruised onto the lot and parked by the shacks across the way.

"I brung out the balloons for Meadlow," Zack fumed, "on account of he looked down at the mouth. But hell, he never even sang."

"He must be tired," I said. "And not feeling well. He's been pushing himself for days."

"Sounds to me like you gone soft on him," Billie said.

"No. It's just . . . well, he seems so driven. I wish I knew how to convince him to ease up on the boy. I think he's a very unhappy man and I feel sorry for him."

She released a low rumbling laugh, like a beer keg rolling down a stairwell. "After the way he just acted, I'd as soon feel sorry for this armadillo. Meadlow, he's all stainless-steel metal inside and out."

"And talk about ugly," Zack said. "I bet his mama had to tie a porkchop around his neck to get the family dog to play with him."

"I want to talk to you, Padre."

The three of us swung our eyes around to where Meadlow lurked just beyond the range of the TV's glaucous light. He might have overheard everything we had said.

"You oughtn't to come creeping up on folks like that," Billie warned him.

"Are you coming or aren't you?"

Since I figured he meant to browbeat me for talking about him behind his back, I didn't care to involve the Horskuses. "Save my place. See you in a minute."

"We'll be here till the white dot disappears," Billie said.

Meadlow made for the cafe. Then, once we were out of sight, he branched off the main path and backtracked behind the stucco shacks.

"What's up?" I asked.

"Shhh! They'll hear you."

"Who? Where are we headed?"

"Shut up. You'll see."

As I hobbled after him, live things skittered around my shoes in the coarse, cutting weeds. I hoped they were lizards or field mice, not snakes. The night had a ceaseless drone, partly from insects, primarily from air conditioners. The buzzing seemed to be inside my head, too, and it threw me off balance. I stumbled once and blamed it on the blisters, but I had drunk six beers, hadn't eaten all day and wasn't at my best. I couldn't understand why Meadlow didn't chew me out here and get it over with.

When we had circled around to the far side of the compound, our shirts soaking with sweat and our cuffs prickly with cockleburs, he grabbed my arm and commanded complete silence. Then he urged me closer to the rear window of one of the cabins, and as I tried to hang back he shoved me face forward against the wall and held me there.

The window was shut and the Venetian blinds had been drawn, but over the chirring of insects and the throaty hum of air conditioners I heard music, and through a missing slat in the blinds I peered into the room. Though the shack was poorly lit and almost opaque with smoke, I spotted four young men in blue jeans and straw cowboy hats seated on the bed, puffing cigars and drinking from Dr Pepper and tequila bottles. Every few seconds they nudged one another, rolled their eyes, yawped and laughed, and passed the bottles again.

"What is this?" I whispered. "We don't belong—"

The bathroom door swung wide, and a heavy-set woman wearing red high heels and nothing else wriggled through the smoke as though slithering from a filthy scrap of underwear. I attempted to squirm free, but Meadlow tightened his grasp, rubbing my face in it.

The woman started to dance, yet seemed not to know how. Although she chewed gum to the beat of the transistorized music, only her ponderous breasts, like swollen bags of shot, swayed with natural rhythm. Noticing red hair as bright as fortified tomato juice and the long pink vibrator, I recognized Darlene.

From one of the men she borrowed a Dr Pepper bottle, made it disappear for a moment, then reproduced it and repeated the trick with the stimulator. Two men hooted and fell back on the bed, howling. The other two, as stunned as I was, stayed mute and upright while Darlene shook her broad soft fanny, which looked like it had been whipped with a waffle iron.

Meadlow had loosened his grip, and as Darlene toiled at her routine I turned to watch him instead of her. The woman's body was absolutely bare, naked in a display beyond mere nakedness. The cowboys ogled it openly, exhorting her toward a final revelation of the flesh, but Meadlow, squinting fiercely, appeared to have trouble figuring things out. One emotion after another swam over his face—bewilderment, curiosity, anger, disgust. Everything except desire. He studied Darlene as if memorizing a wanted poster.

"Sickening," he said. "Illegal, sickening and irrational."

Before his rising anger and voice could betray us, I towed him away from the window.

"Have you ever seen anything like that?" he sputtered.

"No. Never. And I don't want to again. Let's get out of here."

"What are we going to do?"

"Pack up and leave," I said, spotting an excuse to disrupt his schedule.

"But what about that?" He flung an arm toward the cabin.

"There's nothing we can do."

"I'll be goddamned!" He flung his arm a second time and grabbed at an insect. "We have to stop them."

"It's their room. We had no business peeping at them."

"No business! What kind of priest are you?"

"Everybody asks that. I don't know the answer. I just know if you sneak around at night looking into motel rooms you're liable to see what you didn't expect."

"Why, you're as corrupt as they are."

"I'm facing facts. I'm being pragmatic and not imposing my morality. Isn't that what you're always ordering everybody to do? I'm surprised this bothers you, but since it does, the best solution, it seems to me, is to move to a different motel."

"What, and pretend we didn't know about it? The place is nothing but a brothel."

"I suppose it's a lot like most motels. I wish it weren't, but—"

"My God, listen to you!"

"Look, Meadlow, there's no use getting mad at me. You can't change the situation."

"You watch me. Do you realize the damage it would do to my reputation if the wrong people learned I was working in a whorehouse? One slip-up, one cheap irony like that, and the newspapers would crucify me. I'd never get another job."

"Quiet down. No one'll know."

"We know. What about you? Don't you care about your reputation?"

"I don't have one."

"You don't have much of anything, do you, Padre? I'm going right to Billie and Zack and force them to put an end to this." He spun away from me.

"I don't understand," I said, scrambling to catch up. "Why didn't you notice the girls before?"

"I've been busy with the boy."

"But the other times you were here?"

"I haven't used these rooms in months. They weren't here back then."

"But . . . you're making a mistake. We should move. Billie and Zack won't stop just because you say to."

"Then I'll call the police."

"Oh, come on, Meadlow. The Horskuses have enough trouble. They're barely able to stay in business."

"That doesn't give them the right to break the law. Would you accept a lame excuse like that in confession?"

"Have a heart," I panted, my feet in pain. "Why not look the other way one more night and move tomorrow?"

"There's only one way to look in this case. To stay silent is to lie."

"Lie? You don't believe in moral laws. What's a lie to you?"

"It muddles the truth. And I *do* believe in the federal law. If I expect the police to support me, I can't be an accessory to anything like this."

Batting bugs aside, he strode on through the darkness to where Billie and Zack sat in the pool of light cast by the television set, and I wondered whether something more than concern about his professional standing hadn't deepened his anger. Exasperated by the boy, driven close to physical and emotional exhaustion by the effort to break him, he seemed all too eager to take out his frustration on Billie and Zack.

"You're both in big trouble," Meadlow said, stepping in front of the screen.

"No shit," Billie said. "Stand aside so I can see."

"Are you listening?"

"I heard you." Billie stroked the armadillo's armor. "What's ailing your liver?"

"I found out what those women are up to, and it's disgusting and illegal."

"What's illegal about a bunch of pretty girls?"

"Nothing, so long as they keep their clothes on and their legs crossed."

Zack twisted his face, sniffing trouble, and perched on the arm of Billie's chair. But Billie remained as placid as a large pond into which one small rock had been dropped. "Naked is the way we come into this world, Meadlow. You and me and everybody else. It's natural, healthy. Some say beautiful."

"That's a matter of opinion. I'm concerned about my clients."

"You mean that boy you got locked in the room?"

"I mean his parents and all the people who depend on my reputation. Your motel violates state and federal laws. It's an offense to community standards. I want those women out of here tonight."

"What community? Ain't nobody here except us armadillos and them boys over there. They're having fun. I ain't heard a one complain he was offended."

"If you won't put an end to this, I'll call the police."

"Wait a goddamn minute!" Zack said. "You know so much about the law, you fix it to have us condemned. That'd be fine by me. Otherwise, keep your trap shut."

"I'm not going to argue with you. This place is a whorehouse."

"Right you are. But it's an orderly and quiet one." She brandished her fist just beneath his chin. "And I intend to keep it that way."

Meadlow stepped back, not as though intimidated but as if preparing to strike. His rage, already considerable, fed on her defiance. "Are you so dumb you don't understand what I'm saying?"

Billie stirred now like the inexorable turning of the tide. "My friend, folks don't understand each other as good as they think. And they ain't ever as sharp at running things as they'd like to be. You take a no-account thing like nookie. It's been my experience it can cause more trouble than the atom bomb. Men moan when they don't get enough, then sometimes end up bitching when they do. And you got others, like yourself, fond of busting anybody who's having fun. Hell, I quit trying to figure it out. As many girls as are spreading it around for free, I'm still selling it. So I must be providing a public service, is how I look at it. When the trade stays away, I'll shut down. Not before."

"Meadlow, let's drop it," I said. "We can move."

"Tony's talking sense. Pay before you leave, close the door real quiet behind you, and don't bother coming back."

"Easy there, Billie." Zack was on his feet. "I don't like losing nobody's business. There's space here for the bunch of us. Each girl's got her own cuticle. You won't see them unless you look hard."

"That's not the question. I have a mandate from the people who employ me."

"I reckon I have a mandrake as much as the next fella, Meadlow. But I also admire to earn an extra dollar, specially with business bad as it's been. How the hell can you blame us?" Like a rusty radiator, Zack was heating up as he ran on. "You call us illegal and disgusting, but these days every drugstore in the country is selling fornographic books right across the counter. I ain't talking about girlie calendars and titties now. I'm talking about crotch shots and public hair."

Meadlow folded his arms. "Are you finished?"

"Not by a fucking mile. Is it bread you're after? Okay, we'll pay you."

"I wouldn't touch your money."

"Is it a piece of ass you're after? Then be my guest and take your pick of the girls. Darlene's got a trick that'd purely knock your socks off. She ties knots in a silk scarf and stuffs it—"

"Shut up, you old fool." Meadlow shoved him and he flopped down on Billie's lap. The armadillo squirted out from under Zack.

"Hold it right there," Billie said, setting her husband on his feet. "This has gone far enough." She stood up, and it struck me that I had never seen her standing before. It was a startling sight. Well over six feet and almost as wide, she had the voluminous robe draped from her shoulders like a circus tent. "Tony told you, and I'm telling you, Meadlow. Take it easy and enjoy what's left of your life."

"There's too little time left to waste it with the likes of you."

I expected her to erupt, but letting her eyes travel the abbreviated length of his body, she said as gently as her husky voice would permit, "Maybe you are half over the hill. Hell, ain't any of us getting any younger. But you might could try what Zack said. Step across the way and see couldn't one of the girls get your juices going."

Meadlow's face flooded with color. "You are revolting."

"You run on that way one minute longer and I'll rap on your head so hard—"

"Don't you dare threaten me."

"I ain't threatening. I'm telling you."

"I've had enough. I'm making a citizen's arrest."

Zack chuckled. "What are you going to do, carry Billie and me and all the girls and their Johns to town in your Chevy?"

"He ain't carrying me no place," Billie swore. "In fact, if he don't hush, he ain't going to be carrying his head on his shoulders."

"Stand back," Meadlow demanded, dropping into a karate stance. Cocking one arm across his chest, he drew the other back at his ear. "My hands are registered as lethal weapons. I won't use them unless you force me to."

"It don't appear to me like you could pull your pudding with them hands."

Yielding ground grudgingly, Meadlow looked at me. "Tell her I'm serious."

"This is insane," I said. "Break it up."

"I'm going to ring your bell," Billie muttered.

As she advanced, with Zack's encouragement, Meadlow retreated until he had no more room for maneuvering. Using an awning post, he pushed off, hollering a harsh Oriental syllable, and dealt her a chop to the neck. The edge of his hand thwacked like a meat cleaver, but Billie smiled, said "Shee-it" and socked him in the head, whirling him away from the post.

Nimbly, he fell again into his karate stance, thrust a hand at her belly and watched it disappear up to the wrist. He seemed baffled, though not nearly as much as when she began cuffing him with both fists, throwing roundhouse punches that batted his head back and forth until he dropped to his knees, blood flowing from his mouth and nose.

"Had enough?" she asked, looming over him.

His answer was another Oriental outcry, followed by a few fierce cracks at her kneecaps. I heard something pop and saw her teeter and start to fall. From her face I knew she couldn't figure out what was happening, but Meadlow immediately recognized his mistake. Like an unwise woodsman he had miscalculated the angle and couldn't crawl out from under her quick enough.

Billie tumbled on top of him, overwhelming him with wattles of fat. He kicked and wriggled to roll her off, apparently from panic as much as pain, but he didn't have the strength. He shut his eyes, opened his mouth and began yelling, but his cries were lost down the deep echo chamber of her cleavage. By the time Zack and I pulled them apart, Meadlow had blacked out and everyone at the motel had come running.

Zack ordered the girls and their "guests" back to their rooms, and he and Chiquita Banana each grabbed an arm and pried Billie off Meadlow, sledded her body into unit number one and wrestled her into bed. Although babbling and unable to walk alone, she was at least alive.

About the deprogrammer I had grave doubts. His limbs splayed out at odd angles, he lay on the parking lot like one of those frogs that have been squashed to wafer thinness by a truck. But, bending down, I saw that he was breathing, and I attempted to prod and coax him to consciousness. When that proved impossible, I bundled him in my arms and tottered toward shack seven.

At Tiagatha's room, the boy was pounding the door. "Hey, what happened? I heard shouting."

"There's been a fight. Somebody fell on Meadlow and knocked him out."

"This is our chance. Let me out of here."

"I can't now. I'm carrying him. He's hurt bad. He needs help."

"Drop him and get the key." He rattled the doorknob.

I sensed Meadlow's breathing had quickened; he squirmed in the cradle of my arms. "I'd better call a doctor first. I'll be back."

"Please . . ."

As soon as I had stretched Meadlow out on the bed, he revived and began groaning. He rolled his head from side to side and kicked his feet, clicking the leather soles together. Then he let loose a cry, sat up halfway and fell back, rolling his head again. As goose flesh spread over his arms, he tugged a corner of the cover over himself and curled onto his side.

"Who hit me? If that bastard Zack sucker punched me, I'll kill him."

"Don't you remember? You clobbered Billie's knees and she collapsed on top of you."

"It feels like I got decked by a pile driver. My neck and my spine . . ." He moved, then moaned, "Oh, my God." His white face had gone liverish grey, his inflamed eyelids an angrier red.

"You must have wrenched a muscle. Roll over and I'll rub your back."

"Don't touch me." Meadlow seized my wrist. He still had astonishing strength. "Keep your hands at home. I don't like people pawing at me."

"Just trying to help. I'll call a doctor. You may have cracked a rib."

"No!" He grabbed my other wrist and tightened his grip on them both. His blurry eyes focused far to the left of my face. "No doctors and no dope."

"What are you talking about?" I couldn't twist free.

"I don't want some local horse doctor cutting me up for no reason. And if there's something seriously wrong, I refuse to die half out of my head on drugs. I'd rather have full control of my faculties right up till the end."

"You're talking nonsense, Meadlow. You popped something out of joint. That's all."

"I'll be the judge of that!" he shouted, and it cost him dearly. He bit at his lower lip. "Listen close and do what I say. Can I count on you?"

"Of course, but—"

"No buts. And no drugs, not under any circumstances."

"I don't get it."

He squeezed my wrists savagely. "You'd give me a hard time even on my deathbed, wouldn't you?"

"That hurts."

He tossed my hands aside. "I've been meaning to discuss this with you. In case of an emergency somebody has to look after the arrangements. I've willed my body to science, you know, and I can't have some shit-kicking coroner sawing me apart. To be worth bothering about, I have to be in one piece. So the instant my heart stops beating, pack me in ice and ship my body air freight special handling to Los Angeles."

Rubbing my numb wrists, I nodded. Meadlow seemed to have gone mad. Perhaps the pain had sent him into shock. I decided I'd better humor him.

"What's the address? Slow as the mail is these days, you're liable—"

"You'll find that in my wallet. The name of the doctor at U.S.C., the address, instructions how to pack me, everything. Can you handle it?"

"What'll this cost? I don't have much money."

"That's taken care of. Just follow the instructions in my wallet. Call the doctor and tell him I'm on my way. I don't want to wind up in a jar of formaldehyde at Texas A&M. You're the only one I have to depend on. I couldn't trust anyone else."

Had his tone of voice been different, I might have felt deeply touched. But he didn't beg for help. He demanded it in his usual overbearing manner. Still, I agreed to do what he told me. It had been a long time since I'd been able to do anybody a favor, the first time ever that the little man admitted I could serve a purpose, and also the first time in months I'd felt on familiar ground. At the scene of accidents, sickbeds and deathbeds I had always known I was needed and automatically reverted to role.

"Is there anything else I can do for you?" I asked.

"No. Nothing."

"Nobody I should notify?"

"No one."

"There must be somebody. Your friends and family will want to know how you are."

"I told you I don't have any." He spoke without emotion, yet not without poignance. At any rate, the admission touched me.

"How about your home? Your belongings? What'll become of them?"

"I travel light," he said. "Almost everything I own is with me. My bank's on the alert to look after unpaid bills. You might make a note to cut my credit cards in half. And, oh yeah, notify the Avis office I'm through with the Chevy. Otherwise, I'm up to date on everything. I believe in planning ahead. I hate loose ends."

"How about the boy?"

"What about him?"

"Shouldn't we let him go?"

"Is that supposed to be cute?"

"No. If you're hurt, why drag out his misery? And your own?"

Meadlow smiled. Then again, he might have been grimacing in pain. "You haven't learned much about this business, Padre.

He's liable to break any minute. He's been at the brink all day. It's never too late. I'm not in the grave yet."

"I didn't mean you're dying. But until you're feeling better, who'll bring him his food? What if there's an emergency? At least let me have the key."

"Nothing doing."

"I thought you trusted me."

"The key's in my pocket. If you need it, tell me and I'll decide."

His obstinacy nearly got the best of me, but I knew that would be fatal if I wanted to help Tiagatha. "Can I get you anything?" I asked. "A wet washcloth for your eyes?"

"There's a bottle of soda on the bureau. Bring that."

I fetched the bottle, then crouched beside the bed.

"That's all," Meadlow said.

"I'll stay awhile."

"No." Sprinkling soda on his fingers, he patted his eyelids. "I have some serious thinking to do."

"I imagine so. But you shouldn't be alone at a time like this. We could talk."

"About what?"

"Whatever you like. Tell me what's on your mind."

Meadlow smiled. This time there was no doubt about it. "It won't work. I'm not going to make a last-minute confession."

I had been groping my way as I went along, but as always he delighted in pinning me down. "I didn't ask you to confess."

"What are you pushing?"

"I'm not pushing anything." Then I realized there was no use being oblique. "I'm simply reminding you that you have a soul. You've been baptized all those times. You're a Child of God, like the rest of us, and can always come back to Him."

Standing the soda bottle on his stomach, Meadlow growled. "The kid's converted you. You sound just like a Jesus Freak."

"I don't take that as an insult. Not after what I've seen."

"You should. I wouldn't like anyone calling me a freak."

"What could it possibly mean any more? Ever since I got back from Italy, I've seen all sorts of freaks and all kinds of freakish behavior. Everyone's life looks crazy these days when you stand outside staring in, and I guess there's nothing that seems stranger than believing in God. But if you're forced to be one type of freak or another, I'd rather be a Jesus Freak."

"You better hadn't be including me with the goddamn freaks."

"It's only a word, Meadlow."

"Don't try to suck me in. You're not in any position to throw stones. I'd have a hell of a hard time saying what you are."

"A priest."

"A damn peculiar one."

"No, just a bad one."

"But you're still with them. You haven't joined a commune or married a nun or run for political office."

"I don't deserve much credit for staying. I never knew where to go."

"Christ, use your brain. If you lost a lot of weight and gained a little self-confidence, you could—"

"What? Leave the Order and teach Latin at a prep school?"

"Hell, you could do anything. You've got years to find a good job, meet a woman, marry and have a family, like you told me you wanted. Do something with your life. For Chrissake, live!" Meadlow had to stop and steady the bottle on his stomach.

Though he was exhorting me to do precisely what I had hoped to do in six months, some shred of faith or vocational pride now resisted the idea, and I recalled what Tiagatha had said. "You talk like I've committed suicide without dying. But I'm living. I'll admit I've had my doubts whether I was doing much good as a priest, but I'm positive I wouldn't do any good at all as a layman."

"You're certainly not doing me any good. You want to do

me a favor, leave me alone. I mean it. I'm getting one bitch of a headache."

I stood up on my sore feet.

"One last thing," Meadlow called before I closed the door. "Don't pray for me. I'm not kidding. Don't you dare."

I paused at Tiagatha's room, but heard nothing and didn't speak. In my own room the lone sound was the murmur of the air conditioner, as ceaseless in the performance of its duty as those Carmelite nuns who pray night and day so that at every moment all over the world there will be devotion to God.

Once I had undressed and switched off the lamp, I dropped to my knees and added my solitary voice to the world-wide whisper. Prayer was one act the deprogrammer couldn't prevent, one urge he couldn't eradicate. Despite his warning, I was free to pray for him, and in spite of my failures with them, I could also pray for the others. I ended up abjectly repeating a single word: "Jesus, Jesus, Jesus."

IX

I woke early, on top of the covers, fully clothed. Gathering the bedspread around me, I had begun to roll over when I remembered Meadlow and decided I had better check on him. I opened the door to the appalling heat of another day, then had to wait under the awning while my pupils painfully contracted, focusing on the four-armed tire iron in the back of Zack's truck.

The sun, lost in its own brilliance, had bleached the countryside the color of bone meal, and I noticed an ashen figure struggling against the light. It looked like Meadlow, and I thought I must be mistaken. Yet it was the little man, not in his jaunty orange jogging outfit but dressed in khakis and a sleeveless undershirt, limping in a circle around the parking lot. His head was bowed over a small black book, his spine badly bent, his midsection showing a surprising softness.

I trotted out to him. "What are you doing?"

"Reviewing some material." He spoke in a low voice to conserve his strength.

"You should be in bed. What about your back?"

"I felt better after you left. More mobile, anyhow. I've been up all night."

"You need sleep, Meadlow. Your eyes look awful."

"To hell with them. I have work to do. I told you, I hate loose ends."

"But we agreed on the arrangements. Don't you remember?"

"I'm not talking about that. It's the boy."

"The boy?" The sun burned down to the roots of my hair, and the asphalt scorched through my shoes to the soles of my feet.

"I'm going to finish deprogramming him before anything else goes wrong."

"Look, you're in bad shape. If you won't let me call a doctor, at least rest a few days."

"No. Things have to be speeded up. It burns like hell when I speak." He pointed to the spot where his rib cage curved into the soft pot that had burgeoned at his belly. "Who knows what that fat slob did to me? My guts feel all crumpled up. I'm going to finish and fly to L.A. and see my doctor."

"After last night, why would you work here? What if somebody finds out about the girls?"

"You convinced me no one would."

"Still, we better move on before Zack and Billie try to get even."

"Don't worry about that." He gestured with the black book. "I've taken care of them."

"Is that the boy's Bible?" I asked.

He nodded.

"How did you get it? He'd never give it to you."

"I took it."

"What a crummy thing to do."

"I can't be bothered about your scrupulosity. The Bible was his last crutch. It had to go. Without it he's crippled. Considering the emergency measures I'm planning, he shouldn't last another day."

"And you? With the shape you're in, how long do you figure to last?"

"I've thought about that," he admitted, unperturbed. "I should be able to stay on my feet a few more days. After that . . ." He shrugged, then winced. "We'll see. I'm not expecting you to help."

"You bet I won't."

"I mean you don't have to take your turn. I'll leave him alone during your shift and let him mull things over."

"No, I insist on being with him."

"It'll be uncomfortable in there, and I guarantee you there's no chance of turning things around. It's gone too far."

"Let me talk to Tiagatha."

"Suit yourself."

As Meadlow scuffed across the parking lot, the Bible pressed to his chest, I was reminded of an old, infirm priest who walked that way as though checking his heartbeat with his breviary.

"Please," I said. "What could this mean to you now?"

"Everything."

"Can't we talk it over?"

"It hurts to talk. I've got to pace myself."

"Then I'm going to call the police."

"I've told you twenty times, they approve of the deprogramming."

"They don't approve of the girls. They'll close the motel."

"I thought you were worried about Billie and Zack."

"I'm worried more about the boy."

"Too bad. You're a little late. Zack and I have reached an understanding. I warned him not to let you use the phone."

"I don't believe that. Zack and Billie both detest you."

"But they like my money."

Meadlow fumbled the key ring from his pocket, had trouble finding the right one for room six, then even more in inserting it and snapping open the lock. When the door swung wide, warm ripe air rushed over me.

"Go ahead if you're going," he said.

Tiagatha was in his underwear stretched out on the cot, a mandala of sweat radiating around him on the sheet. The door slammed behind me, and the room went dark.

"Are you awake?" I whispered.

"Yes."

"Mind if I turn on the light?"

"It won't work."

I tried the switch anyway. "The bulb's burnt out," I said, sidling through the darkness to a chair. Perspiration was pouring from me. I sat down and waited for it to dry, but it kept running down my arms and legs. The room seemed to contain the heat of the whole summer, of the entire sweltering state, preserved in a packing crate, wrapped in excelsior that might ignite at any moment. "What's wrong with the air conditioner?"

"Meadlow broke it. He pulled out a part, then cut the electricity altogether."

"Why did he do that?"

"Isn't it obvious? He wants to make me as uncomfortable as he can. He came in here late last night, woke me up and said he was tired of playing around. It was time to drop the kid gloves."

"My God, it must be a hundred and twenty." I wiped my face with a shirttail.

"He swiped my Bible, too. Ripped it right out of my hands. When I went to grab it back, he hit me. He punched me three or four times and pushed me into bed."

"Hit you?" I swung around in the chair. "I'll call him in here and—"

"And what? You won't stop him. Nobody will. It's starting now, just like I warned you it would, and he'll just keep turning the screws tighter."

"I'll phone . . . I'll try to phone your parents." I didn't care to admit this was no longer possible. The screws he talked about seemed to be tightening on me as well.

"Why bother? They hired him."

"No, your mother, she'll listen."

"Sure, she'll listen to you, but she'll do what my father says. He's the deprogrammer in our house. Why expect them to step in when you won't? You've got to set me free, or no one will."

"That's impossible." My pleading voice filled the darkness. "We're in a desert. There's nowhere to hide. He'd catch you, and who knows what he'd do to the two of us. He's in a terrible mood, Tiagatha. He might not let me in here any more. Then what kind of help would I be?"

"The same as now. Let me out and I'll take my chances."

"Don't you understand? There's no way to do it."

The cot creaked as he sat up. "Steal the keys to the Chevy and have it running right outside the room tonight. I'll work at prying the boards off one of these windows. I have friends in Corpus Christi who'll hide me."

"I could never get the keys. They're in Meadlow's pocket."

"Then hot-wire the car. Find a piece of aluminum foil and reach up under the dashboard to the ignition wires."

"I don't drive."

"Oh, come on. It's easy. I've done it dozens of times."

"No, I don't know anything about cars."

The boy sagged back on the canvas.

"Don't give up." I dragged the chair closer, but I still couldn't see him. "It won't last much longer, I promise."

"How can you promise? I don't know how long I'll last. When Meadlow came in last night, he was shriveled up like a spider, in awful pain. But he kept picking at me, making noises, poking and shaking me. I know what he's up to. He thinks if he breaks me down physically I won't be able to defend my beliefs."

"But you saw how crippled he is. That's why this won't last. He's sixty-two years old. He can't keep it up."

"I wouldn't count on that. He might get better. Anyway, the situation isn't as simple as I thought. It's not enough for me to hang on and hope. For days I've been telling you that you should act, but here I've been listening to Meadlow blaspheme my beliefs, letting him drag me down to his level. Last night I realized I don't have to swallow whatever he says or does to me. After all, even Christ lost His temper."

"What are you getting at?" I had the sense that a storm was about to break, especially when the air-conditioning duct, buffeted by wind, rumbled like staged thunder.

"Well . . . it's a question of my soul. You couldn't blame me no matter what I did to defend myself."

"What do you have in mind?"

"Nothing particular. Not yet. But even if I killed him, you couldn't—"

"Don't talk that way. This doesn't sound like you."

"These past few days have changed me, Father. When your back's to the wall and nobody'll help, you have to do something."

Again I strained for a glimpse of him. I thought if I could see his eyes I could gauge his seriousness, but the room was far too dark. "Don't be foolish. Meadlow may be sick, but he's not weak. Look how he stole your Bible."

"I don't plan to wrestle him. I'll sneak up from behind and hit him with something. A chair, maybe. Yes, that's what I'll do. Crack him over the head and get out of here before it's too late."

Despite the heat, I shivered and my upper body shed water. "Please don't do this, Tiagatha. I'll find a better way, I swear. Just don't hurt Meadlow."

"Do you care that much about him?"

"I'm worrying more about you. It'd be horrible to have that on your conscience. And if it didn't work he'd rip you apart. I don't want anything to happen to either of you."

"You can't have it both ways, Father. Make up your mind and stop standing around wringing your hands. 'Quit ye like men,' the Bible says."

"Okay, I'm with you. Give me a little more time and I'll come up with an answer."

"How much time? What answer?"

"I've got a few ideas. I need a day to work things out."

"All right, one day. No more."

"Good. Thanks. Trust me." Pawing in the darkness, I found his arm and patted it. "Now, why don't you sleep? Meadlow may bother you again tonight, and you'll be rested."

While Tiagatha rolled over, I sat there open-eyed and wide awake, wondering how I could possibly keep my promise. I considered barricading Meadlow in his room. But how? Or drugging him. Where would I get drugs? Then I thought maybe the little man was more seriously ill than I suspected. What if he died? Was that the only answer? No, desperate as I was, I refused to pray for that.

When the key rattled in the lock, I averted my eyes, expecting to be blinded by sunlight. But as the door swung back the space was filled with hazy grey, and standing in silhouette, Meadlow appeared to be more misshapen than before.

"You two having a séance? Or catching a snooze?"

"What do you expect us to do in this heat?"

"Sweat."

"I want a word with you." I led him outside, tempted to overwhelm him with my ample flesh the way Billie had. "Why did you cut off the electricity?"

"To save energy. I'm an ecologist."

"This is no joke. It's unbearable in there."

"That's how it's supposed to be. In the past I've gotten good results from sensory deprivation. Next to surgery, it's the surest method of behavior modification."

"Sensory deprivation! That's a fancy term for torture."

"What do you mean?" he asked innocently. "I don't even have to touch him."

"Don't lie to me. You hit him last night."

"A synaptic slip-up. He rushed at me and I lost control. It won't happen again. I'll get quicker results by slowly increasing his discomfort, leaving him in the dark, always slightly hungry and tired and disoriented. His own nervous system will do the work for me."

"Why, you're a Nazi, Meadlow."

"Get out of my way." Clamping his hands to my elbows, he squeezed tight, banishing any thought I had of tangling with him. What made the moment more excruciating was that he held his ravaged face a few inches from mine.

"You look like . . ."

"What?" he asked, twisting the truth from me.

Like death, I thought, but said, "Sick. You ought to be in bed."

"I've got a job to finish."

"Then take me," I begged him. "My God, if you won't be satisfied until you've done one more deprogramming, spare the boy and let it be me."

Meadlow laughed—literally in my face. "No challenge, no satisfaction in that. You'll fall of your own weight." He pushed me aside and went into the room.

A strong breeze needled grains of sand into my bare arms and neck. Though great blimplike clouds had scudded up from the south, the heat hadn't diminished and the air felt combustibly dry. I found it hard to believe it would rain, and thought this was what they had here instead—stinging dust storms. As a mesquite branch skittered across the asphalt, scraping out the sound of fingernails on slate, I sprinted through the swirling sand toward the U-Et-Yet Cafe.

Zack had taken a booth by the window and was sitting there

looking as shriveled as Meadlow. He had deep, discolored circles under his eyes and appeared to be counting the liver spots on the back of both his hands.

"Hi, Tony. I seen you chugging across the parking lot. You keeping up your exercises?"

"Just anxious to get in out of the wind."

"Be nice to have some rain, wouldn't it? Might hold the dust down."

I slid into the booth opposite him. "How's Billie?"

"Better than last night. Like something to eat?"

"No, thanks. I haven't been hungry for days."

"Me neither. Too much commotion. Old Billie, she had me awake till dawn crabbing about how she's going to get even with Meadlow."

"I don't blame her. Anytime you and she want to teach him a lesson, I'm with you. The three of us together could take him."

"No way," Zack said. "I talked her out of that. No percentage in it for us."

"You're wrong. Meadlow needs to have somebody pull him up short. Where's Billie now?"

"In bed. She claims she's having dizzy spells on account of that first carrot-y chop your friend gave her."

"He's not my friend. I'm with Billie. I'm going to lose a lot of respect for you if you let him get away with slugging your wife."

"Oh, it hurt her feelings more than anything. She ain't used to getting whipped."

"Still, you should kick him off your property. Make him move from those rooms."

"What, and have him haul ass to the cops and spill his guts about the girls? No way, Tony, no way."

"Don't you understand, he's liable to report you anyhow? He'll always have that hanging over your heads."

"No, I don't reckon he'll do anything."

"Why, because you two made a deal? Because he gave you money to keep me away from the phone? I still wouldn't trust him."

"No, Tony, it ain't just the dough. What I been saying to Billie is we're even-steven now. Sure he's got us by the balls because of the girls, but he's the one responsible for that ruckus last night. He punched her first, and you heard what he said about his hands being registered. So I figure, he threatens to go to the cops about this prostitute business and I'll press charges on him for belting Billie with an illegal weapon. I don't believe she ever will carry her head right after that clout."

I stared out at the parking lot, trying to think of a way to persuade Zack to help. Appeals to his pride and anger hadn't worked, and I didn't have the money to take advantage of his avarice. It occurred to me I was reviewing the list of deadly sins—which was as bad as begging Tiagatha to recant his beliefs or praying for Meadlow's death. There had to be a better way.

The wind had blown long snakes of sand onto the asphalt, and as they circled around and around in a futile chase after their own tails I felt slightly sick. Vertigo seemed to have invaded my brain as well, where something too slippery to be called ideas wormed in and out of my grasp.

"I hate to bring this up when you already have so much on your mind," I said, "but there could be a lot more trouble."

Zack wrinkled his nose. "How's that?"

"What Meadlow's doing to the boy isn't right."

He held up his hand.

"I know. You don't want to hear it. But Meadlow is torturing Tiagatha. He hit him, and he switched off the electricity and the air conditioner and swiped his Bible and won't let him sleep or eat. If anything goes wrong, you're partly responsible because of this arrangement you have with Meadlow."

"What could go wrong?"

"The boy is threatening to kill Meadlow."

Zack threw back his head, stretching his neck taut, and as he chuckled his Adam's apple bobbed up and down. "Fat fucking chance."

"I'm serious. He swore he'd brain Meadlow with a chair."

"I'll still lay my money on Meadlow."

"Normally I would, too, but Billie hurt him bad. He can barely stand up straight." I decided to play my last card. "And if he's half as sick as he looks, you could have a dying man on your hands no matter what the boy does."

Again Zack chuckled.

"It's not funny. Something's the matter with him, not just because of the fight. I can see it in his face. He's like an animal in a trap. If anything happens, you'll have to call in the cops and the coroner, and they'll notice the girls."

"Tony, Tony, you're pulling my chain. You couldn't kill that little cocksucker with a silver bullet."

"But the boy, he—"

"He'll be fine. Meadlow's worked on half a dozen kids here. They're bruised and groggy afterward, but they come through all right. Hell, sometimes their parents drive down to pick them up and it's like Graduation Day. Everybody smiling and shaking hands. No sir, I'm not butting in. Not after last night."

I sagged back in the booth.

"Know what I bet," Zack said. "I bet Meadlow ain't never been laid, and that's why he was mad at us over the girls."

"There are other reasons. I mean, to be honest, I don't approve of what you're doing."

"But being a priest, Tony, you don't understand how it galls a guy not to know the score. I remember way back when my brother Riley told me he'd bought his first piece of poontang. I didn't have any idea what he was talking about. He said he'd walked right up to this gal, asked for what he wanted and got himself two dollars' worth. Hell, I thought poontang was some kind of fishing bait and he lugged it home in a bucket. When I asked old Riley what he caught with it, know what he said?"

I shook my head.

"Crabs!" Zack smacked the Formica-topped table.

I glanced out the window again. Thunderheads were building, darkening, gaining density, and bolts of heat lightning forked through the sky. Then my belly rumbled.

"Starting to thunder," Zack kidded me. He too had turned to look out the window. The girls were strolling across the parking lot, leaning into the wind, their lacquered hairdos waving like nuns' wimples.

"Here they come for their afternoon snack. Some claim they can't work on an empty stomach. Guess I better get behind the grill."

Silent, yawning and sullen, the girls clustered around the cash register like a wilting spray of flowers, their perfume filling the room with a smell that reminded me of funerals. I left and set out through the abrasive wind. From Tiagatha's room I heard voices, assumed Meadlow and the boy were arguing, and had started to steer clear when someone shouted, "Let me go! Don't touch me with that thing!"

"Don't be scared, honey. We're here to have fun," said a silky voice, surely not Meadlow's.

I drifted nearer the door.

"Leave me alone!" Tiagatha cried.

"Why, sonny, your eyes are big as saucers. Ain't you ever seen anything like this? Touch it. It don't have teeth."

"I'm warning you."

"That's the way, big fella. I like my men mean. Mean and red-headed. Look, baby, I got red hair, too. Both places. How about you? Come on and peel out of them silly underpants."

"No! Stop!"

There was a loud *crump,* as if he had leaped onto the cot. Then he slammed into the door and called out for help.

"What's happening?" I hollered.

"There's a naked woman. She won't leave me alone."

"What! Where's Meadlow?"

"I don't know. Get me out of here!"

"Never mind him, lover boy. Let Darlene show you a good time. Wouldn't you like a little loving?" There came a click, then a steady buzzing like that of an electric razor. "See how I do my joy stick? Look how easy it goes in. I'm just melting for you."

The buzz was muffled now, and the boy banged on the door. "Father, please help me."

I banged back. "Stop! Do you hear me? Stop that and open up."

"Oh, I'm open, but I can't stop for nothing," moaned Darlene. "Come on, honey, you do me, then I'll do you."

I pounded and kicked the door. "I said stop! This is Father Amico."

"I don't give a damn if it's Brother Texaco," she snarled. "Bug off, buddy. We're having us a party."

"Listen, you, I'm a priest."

"That's your problem."

"I order you to release that boy."

"I don't take orders from anyone except the man that pays me."

"Was it Meadlow? Did he tell you to do this?"

"That's my business. I don't discuss customers." Then, in a much different tone, "Grab a hold of that, honey, and feel how nice. They're all mine. No foam rubber." A fist smacked against flesh, and Darlene let out a yowl. "Hey, don't get smart with me or I'll break your balls."

Tiagatha lurched away from the door, and it sounded as if they had both landed on the cot.

"Caught you! Save your squirming for later. I like a man with moves."

I leaned a shoulder forward and rammed my full weight against the door, almost paralyzing my spine. But the door didn't budge. Stepping back, I switched to the other shoulder and got the same result.

While I was reeling around in pain, Zack left the cafe carrying a trash can. I called to him and hurried off in his direction.

"Help! You have to help. Darlene's in with the boy."

He kept going toward the dump.

"Don't you hear what I'm saying?"

"I ain't deaf. Quiet down, Tony. It's all over now but the moaning and groaning. Meadlow always gets his man one way or the other. Darlene always gets hers, too."

"Is that why he paid you—not just to guard me, but for the whore?"

I grabbed his arm and he dropped the can. The wind scattered bacon rinds, eggshells and greasy papers.

"What the hell you doing?" He wriggled, but couldn't break free. "Who's going to clean this up?"

"You'd better do something quick."

"Bullshit. You do something. You best pick up that garbage before Billie sees it."

"I'm not going to stand by and let this go on. Don't you understand? I'm a priest. If you won't stop her, I will. I'll call the police."

"Wait a minute. Weren't you a priest last night?"

"Of course."

"Then you're being pretty damn two-faced. When Meadlow said he'd call the cops, you were on our side."

"I wasn't on anybody's side."

"Didn't you tell him not to? Didn't you say it was none of his business? Well, it's none of yours, either. Lemme go or I'll kick you in the nuts."

I pushed the old man an arm's-length away, still holding on

to him. He felt light and loose-limbed as a rag doll, and in my anger I almost shook him apart.

"This is different. The boy doesn't want Darlene."

"Well, he's getting her anyhow, ain't he?"

I cocked my arm to punch him, but Zack didn't flinch.

"Go ahead. Hit me. Take it out on me just because you can't make up your own goddamn mind."

Something snapped inside me, and I let him go.

"What are you doing?" he shouted when I wheeled around and ran off.

"I've made up my mind. I'm going to put an end to this."

I raced to Meadlow's room, flicked on the overhead light and went to the bed, where the little man had curled under the covers.

"Get up."

"Cut that light," he said, "and keep quiet."

"You lousy bastard, you sent that whore in there and you're going to call her off. I won't stand for this, Meadlow."

"Afraid you'll have to." He rolled over and propped himself on an elbow. "It's part of the new schedule."

"That's the most corrupt, rotten, hypocritical . . . Last night you wanted to have that woman arrested."

"Yeah, but you convinced me it's none of my business what goes on in motel rooms. You said to look the other way. That's what I'm doing."

As with Zack, it hurt to have my words flung back in my face. But I leaned my considerable size and weight far forward to remind Meadlow of that instant when Billie had avalanched over him.

"Forget what I said last night. Forget everything except calling off Darlene."

"I never interrupt a deprogramming."

"Deprogramming!" I spat it at him. "I'm sick of the word. Is that what you call hiring a whore to abuse the boy? You could never have broken his beliefs."

"We'll see who breaks first."

"No, you're beaten now no matter what. Because you've become what you claimed to be fighting. You're the one who's irrational."

He threw off the covers and swung his legs over the side of the bed, but I shoved him back. He shuddered in pain, and the satisfaction I got from this left me light-headed.

"You're old, Meadlow, and you're afraid of dying. You hate anyone younger, anyone who's happy, anyone who believes."

"Get out of my room. You keep crowding me and I'm going to lose my temper."

"I'm not leaving until I have the key."

"Get fucked, Padre."

I lunged straight ahead and wrapped my hands around his sinewy neck, thrusting both thumbs against his Adam's apple.

"You have to be kidding." He spoke in a perfectly normal voice. "Are you really that weak?"

I roared, tightening my grip, but Meadlow brushed my hands aside. When I grabbed at him again, he chopped swiftly at my chest, striking a soft spot just below the sternum. All the air rushed out of me, and I staggered back on my heels and sat down hard. I shook my head clear, scrambled upright and came at him once more. This time he caught both my wrists in one hand and slapped my face back and forth with the other.

"Settle down, goddammit, or I'll knock you down."

When I wouldn't stop fighting, that was what he did. With his fist instead of the flat of his palm, he punched me a few times, then let me sink to my knees and slump onto my side, bleeding from the nose and mouth.

"See what you made me do, you damn fool?" he cried out. "Why does everybody have to be so stupid and stubborn?"

I lost consciousness for a few seconds, and when I revived, the room wavered and rocked. At every breath I tasted my own blood and thought I heard it bubble in my ears. Yet my senses were surely betraying me. As Meadlow crawled back into bed,

I couldn't believe this sick, crippled little old man had beaten me so badly.

When things quit spinning, I pulled myself to my feet. "Forget what I promised last night," I said. "I'm not going to look after those arrangements. I hope you die here alone and some hick doctor carves you up like a turkey."

X

I left, and the wind lapped at my shirt and pants. Rather than pass the boy's room, I cut diagonally across the parking lot. Zack called to me from the steps of the cafe, but I licked the blood from my lips and kept on going, stumbling into the fields where scrub brush raked at my clothes and skin.

The first raindrops appeared as tiny eruptions in the caked earth. A *smack,* a puff of dust, and another miniature crater in the sand. I raised my face to the rain, and a bolt of lightning scrawled across the sky. It glowed on my eyeball when I blinked. Then, at a clap of thunder, the clouds cracked open, releasing the downpour, and soon the ground was all the same coppery color.

The sand sucked at my feet. I thought I was walking slowly downhill, then discovered I was on my knees. Scratches criss-crossed my arms and hands. My trousers had been ripped, too, as I came through the cactus and cockleburs, and blood dribbled from the tears and mingled with the raindrops all around me. But after a few nearly sleepless nights and days without food, after too many jolts and then Meadlow's punches, I didn't feel any pain. I wasn't feeling much of anything, in fact, although I realized I had taken a stand at last . . . and been knocked flat.

My first reflex was to close my eyes, but I knew nothing would go away. I myself could go away, but I couldn't delude myself any longer that my disappearance wouldn't matter.

Dragging myself upright, I retraced my steps through the thorns, and by the time I got clear of the thicket it had stopped raining. Steam was rising from puddles on the parking lot. No one was in sight.

My shoes squeaked as I crossed the macadam, and the wheezing of air conditioners engulfed me like a single asthmatic lung. My own respiration was shallow and erratic as I darted a glance at the U-Et-Yet Cafe, then grabbed the rusty tire iron from the back of the pickup truck.

In room six I heard footsteps, deep breathing and Darlene laughing. They might have been running laps around the furniture. Forcing the flat end of the tire iron under the metal flange, I leaned my weight against it, groaning as I strained. The dry wood groaned, too, and cracked as the screwheads snapped off and sent me staggering backward.

The door flew open and Tiagatha tore out, wearing only underpants. Darlene, in the buff, was right behind him, but I stepped between them and raised the tire tool.

"That's far enough."

She cowered back into the room.

"Put on your pants," I told Tiagatha. "Then head for the highway. Flag down a car. Hitchhike. I'll cover you. You said you had friends in Corpus Christi. Go there."

Bleeding from the face and arms, my clothes tattered and drenched, the tire iron in my hand, I must have appeared demented to him, a hulking murderer, not an avenging angel. But there was no time to explain. Darlene had started to yell.

"Go on," I said. "Get your clothes and get out of here."

While I kept the woman cornered, he pulled on his trousers, grabbed his shirt and hotfooted it across the asphalt. Then he doubled back and looked into the pickup truck.

"You forgot your shoes!" I called to him. "Hurry!"

Zack came out of the cafe, screaming. The door to Billie's room opened and she emerged, carrying her head awkwardly, just at the instant Chiquita Banana craned his neck around the door to my room to see what all the noise was about.

"Run for it!" I hollered.

But the boy wasn't listening. The keys must have been in the ignition, or else he had a miraculous touch with a hot wire. He slid behind the steering wheel and the engine kicked over at once. Grinding the gears into reverse, he swung around and roared forward, choked the motor, bucked for a few yards, then gradually accelerated.

Meadlow, in his underpants, raced from room seven in a half-crouch, scuttling sideways, painfully deformed. His outraged cry was the most resonant of all and seemed to act as a signal to the others. They started running. Darlene brushed by me, swaddled in a sheet. Even Billie hobbled as best she could, but was quickly passed by Zack and the Mexican boy. Everybody sprinted for the center of the parking lot.

Meadlow was closest and had the best angle to intercept the truck. Waving his arms, he shrieked, "Stop, you son of a bitch! Stop!" And when he saw Tiagatha had no intention of stopping, he didn't, either. At the last instant, still shouting, he hurled himself headlong, as if he expected to halt the truck with his body. Or more likely he was bluffing, daring the boy to drive over him if he wanted to escape.

It appeared to me Tiagatha had time to brake or swerve, but metal met flesh with a thump, and the bumper took Meadlow's weight, bent, and sent him on a skin-burning slide across the asphalt.Before the boy hit the brake, the truck had caught up to the deprogrammer, crunching him under its front and rear tires. Then it ground to a stop several feet away, the radiator erupting in a geyser of rusty water.

Tiagatha jumped from the pickup, took a terrified look at

Meadlow and headed for the highway, sobbing as he loped through the field. Zack and Billie chased after him but fell farther behind at every stride. Chiquita Banana dashed in the opposite direction, behind me, out of sight.

At this distance the deprogrammer was little more than a white smudge on the blacktop. But as I came closer I saw that he was moving, even though his chest was crushed—the skin bore an almost perfect imprint of the tires—and his legs were twisted as though somebody had sloppily tried to braid them together. One arm had snapped at the shoulder and lay useless, while the other fluttered about in the air.

As he yelled and strained, Meadlow appeared to be performing an isometric contraction, which had the effect of making him seem smaller. His muscles squeezed in upon themselves, wrapping tighter around the bones, and the flesh on his face had fallen into the crevices of his skull.

Seeing me, he said, "Call the cops. I want that boy back."

"Quiet." I crouched beside him, clasping my hands together to stop them from shaking. "Call an ambulance," I told Zack, who had come trotting back from the field and went on past us.

A spasm shot through Meadlow. "No, the cops! They'll catch that bastard."

"Please, you're hurting yourself by screaming."

"Who did this? Who the hell did it?" Despite the pain, the words kept spurting out of him. "You did it, didn't you? You let him loose with that." His good hand swiped at the tire iron. "Get it out of my sight."

I laid it above his head. "Here, let me help you."

"You call this help? Setting him free to run over me?" His cheeks were twitching as he lifted his head and studied the harrowed contours of his physique as some dour farmer might look at a plot that had been reduced to perpetual barrenness. "You miserable fat bastard. Look what you've done." He grabbed my arm and tried to haul himself up.

"Let go, Meadlow. You're hurting yourself."

"You can't hurt me."

"I said you're hurting yourself."

"I'm sick of you feeling sorry for me. I don't want your pity or your prayers."

Squeezing tighter, he started hissing and spitting out unintelligible syllables such as I had never heard, not even when Tiagatha talked in tongues. His left eye clenched with effort, the right remained wide and the pupil wandered.

"Quit this!" I cried. "You're killing yourself."

A shadow swept over us and I glanced up at Billie.

"What's he saying?" she asked.

"I don't know. Have you called an ambulance?"

"Hold on a sec. Let Zack get a good head start."

Behind her I noticed him herding the girls into Meadlow's Chevy.

"We can't wait," I said. "He needs help now."

Yellowish fluid dribbled down Meadlow's chin, and his left eye had rolled open as wide as his right. The red from his lids seemed to bleed into them, then both pupils disappeared. I pried his hand from my arm and laid him back gently.

"He ain't going to make it," Billie murmured. "It ain't an ambulance you'll be wanting."

Suddenly Meadlow's slurred syllables were drowned out by a siren. A squad car careened past the U-Et-Yet Cafe and squealed to a halt, its antenna unlimbering like a fly rod. Locked in the back seat was Tiagatha, a prisoner again.

A Texas Ranger sauntered over, his eyes masked by mirror-lens sunglasses. He had a distinctive two-tone tan, much darker on his left arm and the left side of his face.

"What's happening here?" he asked.

Billie moved between the patrolman and me, and Zack hustled over beside her.

"Howdy, Officer," he said.

"The boy claims he was kidnapped. Says he was held captive here. I thought I'd check whether this is the one Meadlow's working on."

"Sure is. So don't blame it on us. We never brung him here. Meadlow did it."

Zack stood aside then, as if to introduce the officer to the crumpled little man.

"What the hell?" The Ranger dropped a hand to his holster. "Get back from the body and be quick about it."

I didn't move.

"It ain't what it looks like," Zack assured him.

"I'll decide what it looks like. Has there been foul play?"

"There ain't been no play whatsoever," Zack said. "Just an accident. The hippie, he stole my truck and smacked into Meadlow."

"Shut up a minute." Then to me the Ranger repeated, "Everyone away from the body."

"I'm a priest. I haven't finished." I bowed my head close to the deprogrammer's ear, a delicate petal bloodied by his slide across the macadam. "Listen, Meadlow. You don't have to answer, just hear me out. Don't let our arguments stand in the way. You were baptized a Catholic . . ."

Above me, Zack was telling the Ranger, "That's the truth. He's a priest. Father Tony from New York City. Ain't that so, Billie?"

"Sure is."

"If you believe anything at all, don't die without admitting it—to God, not me."

There was no sign and no answer from him, and the silence, the adamant angle of his jaw, upset me more than the first gory sight of him. I would rather he had mocked me as usual, anything to indicate it wasn't too late.

"Please, listen to me." I grabbed his good arm.

The Ranger squatted opposite me, peeled off his sunglasses and held them above Meadlow's nose and mouth. The mirror lenses remained unclouded.

"This man's dead."

I released the arm and was about to stand up when I heard someone racing across the macadam, coming up behind me. It was Chiquita Banana, lugging my black leather travel kit.

"Padre, Padre, mire! Le falta esto?" He handed me the case and knelt next to me.

The Ranger got to his feet. "I want everybody up and over to the squad car. We're going to get this straightened out pronto."

"I told you, I'm not finished."

"What's to finish? This guy's dead."

"Leave me alone." I had no time for a debate about when the soul departed the body or at what point Extreme Unction became useless.

The Ranger folded his arms, waiting for me to show him exactly what I planned to do with a dead man. Billie and Zack waited and watched, too, and Darlene and the girls crowded around as well. Another time—any other time—I might have felt they were observing me with the same condescending curiosity as those tourists in Rome, but my hands grew steady as I touched the familiar containers of oil and heard Chiquita Banana praying in Spanish.

"Who's the Mexican kid?" the Ranger demanded.

"He cleans the rooms," Zack said.

"He have papers?"

"Papers?"

"Don't play dumb with me."

"Shhh," Billie said. "Can't you see Father Tony's praying?"

Extending my right hand over Meadlow's head, I said aloud, "In the name of the Father and the Son and of the Holy Spirit. May any power that the devil has over you be utterly destroyed, as I place my hands on you and call upon the help of the glorious and holy Mother of God, the Virgin Mary, and of her illustrious spouse, Joseph, and of all the holy angels, archangels, patriarchs, prophets, apostles, martyrs, confessors, virgins and all the saints. Amen."

"How about these girls?" the Ranger asked. "What are they doing here?"

"Just passing through," Zack whispered.

"All of them together? Even the one in the sheet?"

"They're show girls. You know, working up an act."

"Yeah, I bet I know what act."

"Didn't Billie warn you once? Show some respect."

Moistening my thumb with oil, I anointed Meadlow's eyes, ears, nostrils, and moved on to his mouth, praying, "May the Lord forgive you by this holy anointing and His most loving mercy whatever sin you have committed by the use of your speech. Amen." I finished by saying the same prayer over his hands and feet, then making the sign of the cross on them in oil.

Chiquita Banana helped me to my feet. My face felt tight and my eyes burned, but there were no tears. When Billie stepped over to support me on the other side, the Mexican boy let go and stripped off his once-white shirt with its crazy-quilt pattern of greasy handprints and draped it over the upper half of Meadlow's body.

"Father Tony, I'd like you to meet Officer Speed," Zack said.

"Save the introductions. I got some questions. I was briefed about Meadlow. But what about the rest of you? You people part of a side show or something?"

"Well, Billie, she's my wife," Zack said. "She was with a carnival once, but we retired to run this motel, and Meadlow, he brung these hippies here to beat them up and—"

"It's a little more complicated than that," I interrupted. "If we could get inside to an air conditioner, I'd explain everything. I'm going to faint if I don't sit down."

Once more I heard something scampering up behind me, but didn't dare turn for fear that in my dizziness I would fall. The baby armadillo, trailing its leash, ambled between my legs, and letting go of me, Billie scooped it up in her arms.

"That's her pet," Zack told the Ranger. "She's raising it for a flowerpot."

Epilogue

Stationed at the side of City Park Road, I stared over the hills toward the lake, where a water-skier, at this distance the size of a water spider, was slaloming from shoreline to shoreline. The whine of the outboard engine came to me occasionally on a wind that had scoured the sky clear and carried through the open windows of my lemon-drop yellow Vega the smell of cedar, sage, mesquite, and something more. It was the scent, the merest hint, of a change in seasons. Though no leaves had turned yellow, the air had the intensity of an early East Coast autumn.

I wore my black clerical suit, and whereas before I had found it fiercely uncomfortable, the Roman collar as tight as a choker, there was now more than enough room inside and I moved about freely. If I continued losing weight, I would soon need a new one.

A Spanish grammar book was propped against the steering wheel, and I studied the conjugation of the verb "to understand." After Latin, French and Italian, it was easy and I could keep one eye on the empty road ahead. Though I had waited over an hour, that was easy, too. Lately, I had met a lot of men who were experts at patience, and they had provided good example.

I felt . . . It would be difficult to describe my emotions. In Texas, with its telescopic distances and dinning silences, serener minds than mine were apt to risk spectacular leaps, logical and otherwise, but I had learned not to try to put names on things.

I was reviewing *comer,* the verb "to eat," when the lean, red-headed boy stepped out of the cedar forest, dressed as before in muddy boots, tan khakis and a grey work shirt. Dropping the grammar book, I clambered from the Vega and called, "Tiagatha."

He tensed as he turned at the waist. One step backward and he would have been in the woods, lost to me. "What do you want?" he asked.

"To talk to you."

"Who's with you?"

"Nobody. I came alone."

"I thought you said you didn't drive."

"I've learned. You were right. There's not much to it."

"What do you want?" he asked once more, his body still strung tight.

"I told you, I'd just like to talk. Can't we come closer so we don't have to shout?"

"There's nothing to say."

"I can say I'm sorry, can't I? That's something that ought to be said. I can ask you to forgive me."

He turned the rest of his body and took a few steps forward. "You don't have to."

"I think I do. And I'd like to."

He half shrugged and hung his head.

"Will you forgive me, Tiagatha?"

"Of course. And thank you for finally freeing me."

"How have you been?" I asked, easing a few steps forward myself.

"Better. It's good to be back."

Raising his head, he was surprised to see me so close.

"Don't be scared," I said. "I won't hurt you."

"You may not hurt people yourself, Father, but things have a way of happening around you."

"I said I'm sorry. I know that's not enough."

"What have you been up to?" he asked, combing his fingers through his beard.

"This and that. A lot of little things. I've only been back in town a few weeks. I was in jail awhile, you know."

"No, I didn't know. After the cops questioned me and took my statement, they were glad to get me out of the way. They haven't called since. I'm surprised they pressed charges on you. After all, they approved of the deprogramming."

"They didn't press charges, but I guess once the newspapers came in, they had to hold me until they got their story straight."

"Too bad you had to go through that."

"Oh, it wasn't bad. As a matter of fact, it gave me a chance to think. For months I've been mulling some questions over, but I never had a spare moment to make up my mind. So when they slapped me in that cell, I sat tight until I reached a few decisions."

I paused, expecting and wanting him to ask what I'd thought about, what I had decided.

"Billie and Zack had a much tougher time than me," I said to fill the silence. "The cops let me go right after I called my pastor and had him put in a word for me. But Billie and Zack, they'll be behind bars two more months. Still, their spirits are high. Last time I talked to him, Zack told me he had no intention of going back into the same business. He said they'll get some insurance money for the truck, and they have another claim in for damages they say Meadlow did to the rooms. What they'd like to do is make the motel over into a reptile farm. They figure they'll draw as much trade with snakes and lizards as with those girls."

Though that coaxed a smile from Tiagatha, he said nothing, and as we gazed down the sloping hills to the lake he seemed not only shy and wary of me but sunk deep in himself.

"All in all"—I labored to keep the conversation alive—"being in jail was a very interesting experience."

"I bet you converted all the cons." He smiled again.

"Not exactly. Nobody asked for religious instructions or the sacraments. But I listened to their stories and wrote a few letters for them. I even helped draft a legal appeal. It was great to know I could help." My palms had moistened, and I rubbed them on my pants. "One other thing I did. The jail had an exercise area, and I worked out every day, skipping rope and lifting weights."

"Yeah, you look like you've lost weight."

"Sixteen pounds. Like Meadlow used to say—"

"What became of that Mexican boy?" he cut in.

"Chiquita Banana? Actually, his name is Roberto Sanchez. They sent him home to Saltillo."

"He's better off there."

"You're probably right, but everybody says wetbacks are always repeaters. I'd sure like to meet him again and apologize and try to explain things. I'm learning Spanish."

"Just so you can talk to him?"

"No. The parish has me working with chicanos in east Austin. An interesting neighborhood. Most of them speak English, of course, but I'd like to be able to say Mass and administer the sacraments in their language. I figure by the end of a year I'll be fluent."

"Have my parents talked to you?" he broke in again. "Did they ask you to come here?"

"No, I've been wanting to see you. I decided to drop by as soon as I got my driver's license. How about you? Have you been in touch with your family?"

"My mother stopped by the commune earlier this week."

"Oh? How did it go?"

"She was pretty upset about everything. She cried most of the time."

"You can't blame her," I said. "None of us expected it to end like it did. Will you see her again?"

"She's supposed to drive out this Saturday."

"What about your father?"

"She said he was upset and sorry, too. He wants to get together and talk things over. But I'll wait to see how he feels in a few weeks."

"I hope it works out." A breeze blew up from the lake, cooling my face and fluttering his beard. "Feels like fall, doesn't it?"

He nodded and seemed not to know what else to say. I didn't either, now that I realized Tiagatha wasn't interested in listening. Contrary to Meadlow's complaints, I had never found it easy to preach.

"Well, I just wanted to say hello. Guess I'd better be heading home. Take care of yourself."

"You too, Father."

When I had started the car, I waved to him, and he waved back, standing there at the roadside, tall, thin and sober, waiting for me to leave so he could begin his meditation. I swung around and drove into the city.

About the Author

Michael Mewshaw was born in Washington, D.C., in 1943. *Earthly Bread* is his fourth novel in six years. He has also written articles and reviews for the Washington *Post* and the New York *Times,* and is a contributing editor of *Texas Monthly Magazine.* In 1968-69 he held a Fulbright Fellowship in Creative Writing, and in 1973 was awarded a grant by the National Endowment for the Arts. He and his wife Linda have lived and traveled extensively in Europe, North Africa and the Middle East. On leave from the University of Texas to work on a new novel, Mr. Mewshaw is in Europe with his wife and son.